Anonymus

Sleep In Jesus And Blessing In Sorrow

Anonymus

Sleep In Jesus And Blessing In Sorrow

ISBN/EAN: 9783742828897

Manufactured in Europe, USA, Canada, Australia, Japa

Cover: Foto ©Andreas Hilbeck / pixelio.de

Manufactured and distributed by brebook publishing software
(www.brebook.com)

Anonymus

Sleep In Jesus And Blessing In Sorrow

'Thy way, not mine, O Lord.'

SLEEP IN JESUS,

AND

BLESSING IN SORROW.

EDITED BY

MRS. HENRY F. BROCK.

'Them which sleep in Jesus will God bring with Him.'—1 THESS. iv. 14.

'And the Lord God will wipe away tears from off all faces,'—ISA. xxv. 8.

'In the Lord's word will I comfort me.'—Ps. lvi 10.

LONDON:
HATCHARDS, PICCADILLY.
1877.

TO

THE GLORY OF GOD,

AND

IN MEMORY OF THE HOLY DEAD.

PREFACE.

THE object of this little volume is not to add to the number of books already published on the same subject, but rather to supplement them, by offering to some of God's sorrowing children a few suggestive thoughts which, '*through comfort of the Scriptures*,' shall reach certain passages of their grief seldom touched upon in works of a similar character. There are broad outlines in sorrow common to all, but they are filled up very differently by different mourners. Some are more acutely sensitive than others, and suffer in secret, through differences of mental temperament, from many hidden springs of pain for which they cannot claim the common sympathy of their fellow-Christians. There are many folds to their sorrow. But as the word of God shows us that the grace of God is also '*manifold*,' we feel that it can supply *all* our need in Christ Jesus. When God shall comfort Zion, He says that He will comfort '*all her waste places.*' Moreover, it is of His kindness that He sends much of His comfort through the channel of human sympathy, for there are many minds that are cast in the same mould; and St. Paul teaches us, that if one member of the family of Christ is comforted in '*any* trouble,' it is for the 'consolation and salvation of the others' (2 Cor. i. 3–7). The heart, it is true, knoweth its own bitterness, and a stranger may not enter into its secret recesses; but 'a brother is born

for adversity,' and his voice brings timely
relief through the sweetness of that comfort 'wherewith he himself has been comforted of God.'

The selections in prose and verse* that
refer to the present condition of them that
'sleep in Jesus' are fewer in number than
those which refer to the 'blessing in
sorrow :' for this reason, that very little is
revealed in Scripture of the one, and a
great deal is said about the other.

> 'My knowledge of that life is small,
>   The eye of faith is dim,
> But 'tis enough that Christ knows all,
>   And I shall be with Him.'

We would not restrain the power of a
sanctified imagination to soothe our broken
spirits by those sweet strains which sing of

* Selected chiefly from modern authors, by their
kind permission.

a 'land that is fairer than day,' and of the 'bright-faced kindred' there ; but it is not well to lie entranced by their melodies while God is calling us to the stern realities of pain and the solemnities of blessing in sorrow.

It is a golden saying, that 'when spirits are finely touched it is for finest issues.' Thus it is that they who read the Cross aright are less anxious for comfort than for profit in their afflictions. They know that in the spiritual order of His purpose, Who hath washed them from their sins in His own blood, suffering comes first among the 'all things' that work together for the promised 'good' of conformity to the image of the Son (Rom. viii. 28, 29). It is the work of fusion that gives the colour and form to the delicate beauty of the enamel, and it is in the furnace of

affliction that the fairest graces of holiness
are wrought into the believing soul. 'Before I was afflicted I went astray, but now
have I kept Thy word.'

God give His blessing to this little book,
and may it be, in His hands, to many of
His children, the right book at the right
time, for Jesus' sake.

Christ Church Vicarage.
Doncaster.
Easter 1877.

SLEEP IN JESUS,

AND

BLESSING IN SORROW.

THEY are all gone into the world of light,
　And I alone sit lingering here ;
Their very memory is fair and bright,
　And my sad thoughts do clear.

I see them walking in an air of glory,
　Whose light doth trample on my days—
My days which are, at best, but dull and hoary,
　Mere glimmerings and decays.

Dear, beauteous Death, the jewel of the just !
　Shining nowhere but in the dark ;
What mysteries do lie beyond thy dust,
　Could man outlook that mark !

B

He that found some fledged bird's nest may know
  At first sight if the bird be flown,
But what dell or grove he sings in now
  That is to him unknown.

And yet, as angels in some brighter dreams
  Call to the soul when man doth sleep,
So some strange thoughts transcend our troubled
    themes,
  And into glory peep.

If a star were confined into a tomb
  Her captive flames must needs burn there,
But when the hand that locked her up gives room
  She'll shine through all the sphere.

O Father of created life, and all
  Created glories under Thee,
Resume Thy spirit from this world of thrall,
  Into true liberty !

Either disperse these mists which blot and fill
  My perspective still as they pass ;
Or else remove me hence unto that hill
  Where I shall need no glass.

              HENRY VAUGHAN. 1650.

WHAT IS IT TO DIE IN
THE LORD?

It is the last act on earth of *being* in the Lord.
It is to close our Christian race as we began it,
and as we ran it—it is to be found when the
messenger of death comes for us, just where
every call of duty, every trying providence,
every temptation, every mercy, ever since we
began the life of faith, found us—*in Christ.* It
is not the getting into some new shelter ; it is not
the putting on some new armour ; it is not the
coming of the Christian into some new relation
to Christ. It is the enduring to the end of a
relation formed when the Christian life began.
It is the Christian going through the valley of
the shadow of death precisely as he went
through the dangers and trials, and sorrows
and duties, of. this mortal life, saying, 'The
Lord is my Shepherd, I shall not want.' It

is faith overcoming in the last conflict, precisely as it overcame in every previous conflict
of the Christian's pilgrimage. It is the child
of God falling asleep in the same arms of redeeming love in which he was always embraced,
and where he always was safe, in the peace of
God.'

BISHOP M'ILVAINE.

From *The Truth and the Life.*

O JESUS, Lord, the Crucified !
Now let the cross more welcome be ;
Nor let my soul complaining toss,
But plant Thou such a heart in me,
As patiently shall look to Thee
For gain up yonder for my loss.

SCHMOLK.

THEY were—
But what avails it now to tell of what has been?
   Fond-hearted, dear, and passing fair
    As e'er on earth were seen.

They are—
In safety with their God, secure from sin and
    care ;
   And the bright day cannot be far
    When we shall meet them there.

The tears
Their loss might claim, thoughts of their gain
    do dry,
   That we may watch till Christ appears,
    Bringing them in the sky.

Jesus,
Their hope in death, our hope in grief and pain,
   We live in Thee—live Thou in us,
    And all shall meet again !

DR. MONSELL.

. . . . I⟍ is a beautiful thing to see a Christian die. The confession, whilst there is strength to articulate that God is faithful to His promises; the faint pressure of the hand, giving the same testimony when the tongue can no longer do its office; the motion of the lips, inducing you to bend down so that you catch broken syllables of expressions such as these, 'Come, Lord Jesus, come:' these make the chamber in which the righteous die one of the most privileged scenes upon earth; and he that can be present, and gather no assurance that Death is manacled and fettered even whilst grasping the believer, must be either inaccessible to moral evidence, or insensible to the most heart-touching appeal.

REV. H. MELVILLE.

WHY should we fear to die?
Has joy no fallen blossoms here?
Has love no tear, no wintry hour
Of loss and stain, that we should need
No promise of an after-scene
To this poor life?   Ah! rather say   ·
That here it is but night—a night
That waiteth for the coming day,
A vigil to the heavenly morn.
What though the darkness be illumed
By moon and star, by faith and prayer,
Though comrades' hearts be firm and true,
Whose songs make sweet the midnight air,
Still it is night, with watches chill,
And weary strivings with the foe.
Yet courage, for the night is spent—
The sky is breaking on the eastern hills,
And soon the matin call shall rise
Upon our listening ear.   Then, Death,
The handmaid of our soul's true bliss,

With friendly office shall withdraw
The closèd curtains, and unbar
The prison shutters, while the light
Of Immortality pours in,
Which wakes us to the Eternal Day.
Why should we fear to die?

LET us now look upon ourselves as travellers,
and make account that whatever burden God is
pleased to lay upon us He may, perhaps, not
take it off till it come to our time to take up our
lodging in the grave. If He discharge us of it
sooner, let us acknowledge His mercy; but let
us be sure that we discharge not our patience
before God discharges our burden.

BISHOP HOPKINS.

. . . . GOD gives us no suffering, but, as it were, in spite of Himself. His Fatherly love seeks not our pain; but He wounds us to the quick in order that He may cure the evil of our nature. It is needful that He should take from us that which we love wrongly, or which we love so as to interfere with our love to Him. He makes us weep like children from whom the knife with which they are playing is taken away, lest they should kill themselves with it. We weep; we cry aloud in our distress; we are ready to murmur against Him as children in their passion cry out against their own mother. But God lets us weep, and saves us. He afflicts us only for our correction. That for which we are now weeping might have made us weep eternally: that which we now think lost, was truly lost to us had it remained in our possession. God has put it away in safety, that so He may restore it to us in that eternal life

to which we are drawing near. He deprives
us of that which we love in order to enable us
to love it with a purer affection, and to ensure
to us the eternal enjoyment of our treasure in
His own bosom, making us there a hundred-
fold happier than we could ever, of ourselves,
have even desired.

From *Christian Counsels*.
Selections from *Fénélon*. Translated by A. M. JAMES.

THE bereaved soul goes across the border of
Time in quest of the departed spirit, and so
acquaints itself better with Eternity and its
unseen realities. How real is the distant Isle
to which a beloved one has gone, though it
seemed formerly but a dim fog on the sea!
One that I love is there! How real is Eternity
now! Our hearts have now a local habitation
there.

ANON.

'GONE BEFORE.'

Gone, gone—but gone before !
   Silent thy name
Upon the lips where once
   Its music came.

Now the sweet cadence falls
   On heavenly air,
Angels are sounding those
   Syllables fair.

Gone, gone—but gone before !
   No tears can rise,
To dim the light of those
   Immortal eyes.

Nevermore cloud can pass
   Or stain endure,
Upon thy soul redeemed,
   Perfect and pure.

High amid star-like saints,
  Radiant and calm,
Girded with golden harp,
  Bearing green palm :

Bend from the battlements
  Thy shining brow ;
O thou Belovèd One,
  Watch for me now !

Almost I see thee, thou
  Seemest so nigh,
When I look trustfully
  Up to God's sky ;

To the pale tender blue,
  Rippled all o'er,
With the ribbed cloudlets, like
  Sands on a shore.

Oh ! could I drive my bark
  In on that tide,
Leap on the golden sands,
  Spring to thy side !—

They who are one in Christ,
    Hid in His heart,
Death cannot sever, nor
    Hold long apart.

Soon they clasp hands again,
    All partings o'er,
Where the Life-Giver has
    Gone on before.

                    C. NOEL.

            From *The Name of Jesus.*

SUFFERING is Christ's problem to the meek and
lowly in His school. Joy is the solution which
Heaven shall make plain to all waiting souls.
That was a frail and weakly tenement which
rocked upon the waters of the Nile, but it
contained a sleeping prophet and deliverer.
Despise not, then, thy sorrow, O human soul!
for a blessing sleeps within it; and out of it, in
God's 'due season,' shall arise that which shall
teach, and comfort, and save.

'After the power of an endless life.'—*Heb*. vii. 16.

THIS word, 'power,' we are told by Scripture commentators, expresses the immeasurable superiority of Christ's Priesthood over the priesthood of Aaron—the word '*power*' being emphatic, as opposed to the preceding words, 'law' and 'commandment,' which expressed the limitations under which the priests of Aaron acted, and the basis of their authority. The Priesthood of Christ is based on His own inherent qualifications, which flow forth from His own *eternal livingness*. This is in harmony with the teaching of Heb. i. 3, 'Who, *by Himself*, purged our sins.' Here, indeed, is a fount of blessing for every believer in Jesus. That which is true of Christ infinitely is true of the feeblest believers, according to their measure and degree. Through the Blood and Intercession of Jesus they have received 'the power of an endless life.' They live a life which cannot die, because it is the life of Jesus

—a life which, as St. Paul tells us (2 Cor. iv. 11),
is made manifest in their mortal bodies, and
renewed day by day while the outward man is
perishing. Do we Christians sufficiently realise
this? Do we know, by precious experience,
that every peril, every decay of this outward
life, does but strengthen in us that *inward* man,
which is risen with Christ? According to our
faith, so shall it be in this as in other matters of
the kingdom. Oh I the power of the endless
life, which comes to us in the darkest night of
our afflictions, and reveals to us the star-depths
of God's most precious promises! 'Because I
live, ye shall live also.' And when the time
comes, as come it must, when the earthly house
shall be dissolved, 'for this cause we faint not,
knowing that we have a building of God, a
house not made with hands, eternal in the
heavens.' Thank God, we have seen and seen
again the reality of this truth in the peace unutterable which attends our Christian deathbeds.
'The power of an endless life' is then fully
manifested, as a light that shineth more and

more unto the perfect day. When *our* faith
grows weak and our hope dim, let us think of
that glorious cloud of witnesses, 'a cloud
gathering from all lands, and rising like the
morning, at once from the east and from the
west, from the north and from the south.'—
Ps. cvii. 3.

Let us select one from among these many
witnesses, and bless God while we read :—

'. . . . I think,' said that holy man Dr.
Edward Payson, during the last hours of a long
illness, 'the happiness I enjoy is similar to that
enjoyed by glorified spirits before the resurrection. When I used to read Bunyan's description
of the land of Beulah, where the sun shines and
the birds sing day and night, I doubted whether
there was such a place ; but now, my own experience has convinced me of it, and it infinitely
transcends all my previous conceptions.'

Again, when writing to a sister : 'Were I to
adopt the figurative language of Bunyan I might
date this letter from the land of Beulah, of which
I have been for some weeks a happy inhabitant.

The celestial city is full in my view. Its glories beam upon me, its breezes fan me, its odours are wafted to me, its sounds strike upon my ears, and its spirit is breathed into my heart. Nothing separates me from it but the river of death, which now appears but as an insignificant rill which may be crossed at a single step whenever God shall give permission. The Sun of Righteousness has been gradually drawing nearer and nearer, appearing larger and brighter as He approached; and now He fills the whole hemisphere, pouring forth a flood of glory, in which I seem to float like an insect in the beams of the sun—exulting, yet almost trembling, while I gaze on this excessive brightness, and wondering with unutterable wonder why God should thus deign to shine upon a sinful worm. A single heart and a single tongue seem altogether inadequate to my wants. I want a whole heart for every separate emotion, and a whole tongue to express that emotion. But why do I speak thus of myself and of my feelings? Why not speak only of our God and Redeemer? It is

c

because I know not what to say. When I
would speak of Him my words are all swallowed
up. I can only tell you what effects His presence produces, and even of that I can tell you
but little. Could you but know what awaits the
Christian, could you know only as much as I
know, you would not refrain from rejoicing, and
even leaping for joy. Labours, trials, conflicts,
would be nothing. You would rejoice in afflictions, and glory in tribulations, and, like Paul
and Silas, sing God's praise in the darkest night
and in the deepest dungeon. . . . .'

When we read this testimony to God's faithfulness our hearts glow within us. Dear reader,
let this emotion deepen into a motive power,
impelling us to seek, *by constant abiding in
Jesus*, that 'power of an endless life,' which is
equally all-sufficient for life as for death, en-
abling us even *now*, in the midst of the daily
conflict and the daily cares, to say, 'Our sun
does not go down, neither does our moon withdraw itself; for God is our Everlasting Light,
and the days of our mourning are ended.'

THE SOUL'S MEDITATION ON THE LIFE IN GOD AND CHRIST.

THOU who wouldst celebrate
  The Church's solemn days,
Turn thee from earth's corrupt estate,
  Cease from forbidden ways ;
Nor let the mind stray forth to this life's
    tangled maze,
      But self-collected dwell,
      Barring her citadel
From inroads of the low corporeal sense,
To search her hidden life in quiet confidence.

Here, while thy soul finds rest
  Beside the eternal shore,
How in such moments shalt thou best
  Thy Lord and God adore?
How at the throne of grace thy heart's full
    offering pour?
      Let memory and free-will
      Their work of love fulfil,

While reason's highest gifts their Author own,
And with united powers rejoice in God alone.

> What treasure of delight
>> To seek Him and to know!
> Has sin obscured thy mortal sight?
>> Repentant tears must flow,
> And aye implore thy Lord His hidden face to
> show :—
>>> Then bring each hope and fear
>>> Into His presence near :
> Be good or evil, joys or sorrows, thine,
> Refer them all to God, trust thou His arm divine.

> Bid faithful memory trace
>> All her good Lord has given,—
> Marvels of nature, gifts of grace,
>> Sure promises of Heaven,
> Redemption for the lost, and bliss to souls
> forgiven :—
>>> Think of that destined woe
>>> Thy sin should undergo :
> Each bitter torment Christ thy Saviour bore,
> So thou, preserved from wrath, might'st joy for
> evermore.

This all-transcending theme
   With ardour fire thy breast !
Then onward trace God's mercy-scheme,
   Consider of the blest,—
What is their endless peace ? how joy the saints
   at rest ?
       The while thy senses lie
       Entranced in ecstasy,
Let the free spirit heavenward soar in flight,
And come in vision near to Salem's peaceful
   height !

O couldst thou grasp in thought
   The joy God's people share,
When all that loving hearts have sought
   They find in fullness there ;
Freed from their former ills, the weakness and
   the care—
       Within,—without,—around,—
       In glory they abound ;—
Such the full stream for blessèd saints that
   flows,
Where the Great Source of all, Himself in pre-
   sence shows !

Unveilèd, face to face,
　　Him whom they love they see,—
　　And taste the riches of His grace
　　　With all love's fervency ;—
Absorbed in God alone each thought and
　　faculty.
　　　　Aye in the Father's sight
　　　　Christ's visage shineth bright,
True Light that lighteth each one here below,
That gives to Powers above all things at will to
　　know.

　　　Jerusalem in Heaven !
　　　　What gladness must be thine,
　　　Where to the pure of heart is given
　　　　To see the Sight divine,—
Their glory and their crown, one God in Per-
　　sons Trine.
　　　　O Majesty ! how fair !
　　　　O Love that dwellest there,
For happy souls of men and angels bright,
Knit by their Lord in one, for ever in His
　　Light !

How with their might they sing,
    Those blessèd ones on high,
To God their Father and their King,—
    ·One glorious company,
Whose action all is praise, praise one sweet
    melody :—
        The whilst this sole employ
        Compriseth every joy,—
With full fruition of the Godhead blest,
Their bliss ineffable is perfectness of rest.

Does not thy spirit yearn,
    Transported with amaze ?
Wilt thou of these bright singers learn
    To make thy festal days,
In rest or movement, all subserve thy Maker's
    praise ?
        Tell o'er His blessings past,
        Mercies for aye to last ;—
With heart and voice uplifted to the throne,
Praise Him with all thy strength, Him magnify
    alone !

Thrice happy they and wise,
  Who, deaf to fleshly call,
Send up their hearts in sacrifice
  To the great Lord of all ;—
Nor suffer earth's vain cares to mar their festival.
    A servile world in vain
    Would join them to her train ;—
No festive joys for them but Christ hath share,
And in each hallowed fast with their dear Lord
  they fare.

  O grant us of Thy grace,
    Father of Lights ! we pray,
  In this our mortal trial space
    Like service here to pay,—
To hymn Thy glorious Name, to love Thee, and
  obey ;—
    That when on earth below
    Our anthems cease to flow,
Us to Thy Heavenly Kingdom Thou may'st bring,
There with the, Angelic Choir Thine endless
  praise to sing !   Amen.

  (From the Latin of *In Diebus Celebribus*,
  No. 248 in Mone's Collection of Latin Hymns.
  Translated by D. T. Morgan.)

. . . . THAT instrument will make no music that hath but some strings in tune. If, when God strikes on the string of joy or gladness we answer pleasantly, but when He touches upon that of sorrow or humiliation we suit it not, we are broken instruments that make no melody unto God. A well-tuned heart must have all its strings—all its affections ready to answer every touch of God's finger. He will make everything beautiful in its time. Sweet harmony cometh out of some discords.

. . . . Oh ! that we could in all our trials lay ourselves down in these arms of the Almighty— His all-sufficiency in power and goodness. Oh ! how much of the haven should we have in our voyage—how much of home in our pilgrimage —how much of heaven in this wretched earth !

OWEN.

' His children rise up and call him blessed.'

Prov. xxx. 23.

BLESSED art thou ! for never more
Thy fainting soul can weep again ;
Thy cry of sore distress is o'er,
·For where thou art is no more pain.

Blessed art thou ! thy weary feet
Are where the living waters flow ;
For thee no glare of sultry heat,
For thee no chilling touch of snow.

Blessed art thou ! no storm can blow
Where the rough waves have landed thee ;
We toil in rowing, but we know
That where thou art is no more sea.

Blessed art thou ! the heavenly bread
To fill thy yearning soul is given ;
For He on earth Who thousands fed,
Now feeds thee with the joys of Heaven.

Blessed art thou ! redeeming grace
Has cheered thee when with anguish worn,
And now thine eyes have seen His face
Who wore for thee the crown of thorn.

Blest was thine end ! all joyfully
Thy faithful spirit heard the voice, —
' The Master comes and calls for thee,
That where He is thou may'st rejoice.'

No cloud was there, no sound of woe,
But peace, unearthly, pure and deep—
We knew thou wert with Christ ; for, ' so
He giveth His belovèd sleep.'

L. A. B.

' DEATH emptieth the house, but
Not the heart ;
That keeps its treasure safe,
Though out of sight.'

GERALD MASSEY.

'Then shall be brought to pass the saying that is written,
Death is swallowed up in victory.'—1 *Cor.* xv. 54.

IT is a law of our nature that we are, all of
us, intensely interested in each other's history;
and if it concerns us to inquire how a fellow-
man lives, still more deeply anxious are we to
know how he *dies.* There are few (if any) of us
who are so indifferent to the soul's supreme
welfare as to put down the records of a good
man's death without the wish or prayer, 'Let
my last end be like his!' while there are many
sincere Christians who, shrinking from the
thought of death and the grave, find comfort
and strength in those records, as proving that
'He is faithful that promised.'

And if the faithfulness of the Promiser is
tested when the departure from life is short and
peaceful, when death comes as sleep to tired
eyes, when

> ' One beating pulse, one feeble struggle o'er,
> May open wide the everlasting door;'

how shall it not be tried and proved when the
believer is called to pass through the fiery
baptism of martyrdom! And how shall not
we thank God and take courage, when we see
that even a cruel death can be *swallowed up in
victory!* In the records of the 'noble army of
martyrs' we see that the 'sleep in Jesus' is
still possible in the midst of those scenes of
fierce passion and violence which fill our earth
with shame and sorrow. Without is the darkness of the tempest-strife; within, the celestial
calm of a golden sunset. Where can we find
a nobler instance than in the persecutions of
the Christian converts in Madagascar, 1849?
Who can read unmoved the native account of
that martyrdom, which concludes with these
touching words?—

' *Then they prayed:* " *O Lord, receive our spirits, for
Thy love to us has caused this to come upon us; and lay not
this sin to their charge.*" *Thus prayed they as long as they
had any life, and then they died—softly, gently; and there
was at the time a rainbow in the heavens, which seemed
touch the place of the burning.*'

And these are not without successors. Nearer
our own day, in the year 1864, we read the same
records of 'the victory that overcometh' in the
graves of our missionaries in the Melanesian
Islands. Our souls are stirred within us while
we read the narrative given by Bishop Patteson
of the painful death of two of his converts there
—so soon, alas! to be followed by his own
martyrdom. In the case of each and all we
see how 'God giveth His beloved sleep' in
the midst of cruel surroundings from savage
violence :—

'Two very dear youths,' the Bishop writes, 'Norfolk
Islanders, have been taken from me. Fisher Young,
aged 18, and Edwin Nobbs, 22, died of lock-jaw, in
consequence of arrow-wounds received on August 15 at
Santa Cruz Island. God has been very merciful to me.
Their purity, and truthfulness, and gentleness, and self-
denial, their real and simple devotion, are now my best
and truest comforts. Their patient endurance of great
sufferings—for it is an agonising death to die—their
simple trust in God through Christ—their thankful,
happy, holy disposition—shone out brightly through all.
Nothing had power to disquiet them ; nothing could cast
a cloud upon their sunny-bright Christian spirit. One

allusion to our Lord's sufferings, when they were agonised by thirst and fearful convulsions—one prayer or verse of Scripture—always calmed them, always brought that soft, beautiful smile on their dear faces. There was not one word of complaint, *it was all perfect peace.* "Tell my father," said Fisher, "that I was in the path of duty, and he will be so glad. *Poor Santa Cruz people!*" "Ah, my dear boy, you will do more for their conversion by your death than we shall ever do by our lives." I never witnessed anything like it; just when the world, the flesh, and the devil are, in most cases, beginning their work, here was that dear lad as holy and devout as an aged, matured Christian. I need not say that I nursed him night and day with love and reverence. The last night he said, faintly (his body being then rigid as a bar of iron), "Kiss me, Bishop!" At 4 a.m. he started as if from a trance—he had been wandering a good deal, but all his words, even then, were of things pure and holy. His eyes met mine, and I saw the conscious-ness gradually coming back into them. "They never stop singing there, do they?"—for his thoughts were with the angels in heaven. Then he fell asleep. It was not till four days after this that the symptoms came on in Edwin's case. It was not so acute, but far more trying to him. For eight days his jaw was locked; for five days and nights he never slept one instant, spasms continually recurring. He may be said almost literally to have spent the whole time in unwearied prayer and *praise.* "Lovely and pleasant in their lives, and in their death they were not divided."'

It will be well for us to pause and observe
in these touching narratives that the 'sleep in
Jesus' was preceded by the '*mind*,' which was
also 'in Christ Jesus,' for we notice that the
death of these martyrs closely followed upon
their prayers for the forgiveness of their enemies.

'Their patient endurance of great suffering,' writes the
Bishop, some months after, 'and their simple, loving
thought and prayers for their poor Santa Cruz people,
are—and ever, I trust, will be—a holy example before my
eyes. Oh, how blessed to think we are journeying on to
join that blessed company!'

Seven years later were these words fulfilled,
when, on the same rocky island and by the
same savage force, the good Bishop himself laid
down his life for Christ. Steadfast for Christ,
full of courage and faith, and with one only
object, of doing all to the glory of God, he had
encountered peril after peril in the pursuance of
his high and holy work : always at his post, and
conscious only of one desire, that of winning for
Christ the multitudes of Melanesia, scattered as
sheep amidst a thousand isles. How largely he

partook of the spirit of his Saviour may be known from a few words taken from his letters :—

'Those nights when I lie down in a long hut among forty or fifty naked men—cannibals—the only Christian in the island, are the times for me to pour out the soul in prayer and supplication that *they*—those dark, wild heathen about me—may be turned from Satan unto God. And now to me it is permitted to hold up the weak, heal the sick, bind up the broken, "*bring again the outcasts and the lost*"—those wonderful, beautiful words !'

The life he had lived in the spirit of self-sacrifice and martyrdom was a constant preparation for the end.

'It is probably no exaggeration,' writes his friend, 'to say that the faith and love which enabled the first martyr, St. Stephen, not only to pray for his murderers, but to see fully revealed the glory which awaited him, was also his. Hence, as he too fell asleep, the absence of any sign of agony or terror, and the expression of peace which reigned supreme in that sweet smile.'

Let us read the brief but touching record that precedes these words :—

'As they pulled once more alongside the vessel, they murmured but one word, "The body !" Yes, our dear Bishop's body, wrapped carefully in native matting and

D

tied at the neck and ankles. A *palm* frond was thrust into the breast. On removing the matting, the right side of the skull was found to be shattered, the top of the head being cloven with some sharp weapon, whilst about the body were numerous arrow-wounds. Beside all this havoc and ruin the sweet face still smiled; the eyes closed, as if the patient martyr had had time to breathe a prayer for these his murderers. There was no sign of agony or terror. *Peace reigned supreme* in that sweet smile, which will ever live in our remembrance as the last silent blessing of our revered Bishop and beloved friend." *

'Wherefore,' dear reader, 'seeing that we also are compassed about with so great a cloud of witnesses, let *us* lay aside every weight, and the sin which doth so easily beset us, and let us run with patience the race that is set before us, looking unto Jesus, the Author and Finisher of our faith.'

WHEN afflicted, love can allow thee to groan, but not to grumble.—GURNALL.

---

* From *The Life of Bishop Patteson*.

'So He giveth His beloved sleep.'—*Ps*. cxxvii. 2.

HE lay; and a smile was on his face,
Affection over him bent to trace
The token Mercy had left to tell
That with the spirit all was well.

It was the smile that marks the blest;
It told that in hope he had sunk to rest,
Of a joyful rising after his sleep,
No more to suffer, no more to weep.

It spoke of forgiveness of all his foes,
It spoke oblivion of life's long woes,
It spoke firm trust in the Saviour nigh,
It breathed strange whispers of days gone by.

Bliss, as I gazed, o'er grief prevailed;
Not as one without hope my loss I wailed;
I knew *that* body should rise again,
As the soul immortal, and free from stain.

I felt that however long to me
The slumbers of the grave might be,
I should know him again 'mid the countless
    throng
Who shall bear their part in the seraphim's
    song.

Not by the look that he wore in life,
While his spirit was tired with the cruel strife,
That left him only with parting breath,
But by that sweet look he wore in *death*.

ANON.

BURY his body, but embalm his example, and
let it diffuse its fragrance among you from generation to generation.   Call him blessed, and
endeavour to be like him—like him in piety,
in charity, in friendship, in courteousness, in
temper, in conduct, in word and deed.

BISHOP HORNE.

' He asked life of thee, and thou gavest him a long life,
　　even for ever and ever.'—*Ps.* xxi. 4.

' HE is not dead,' but only lieth sleeping
　In the sweet refuge of his Master's breast ;
And far away from sorrow, toil, and weeping :
　' He is not dead,' but only taking rest.

What though the highest hopes he dearly
　　cherished
　All faded gently as the setting sun ;
What though our own fond expectations perished
　Ere yet life's noblest labour seemed begun ;

What though he standeth at no earthly altar ;
　Yet in white raiment, on the golden floor,
Where love is perfect, and no step can falter,
　He serveth as a Priest for evermore !

Oh ! glorious end of life's short day of sadness !
　Oh ! blessed course so well and nobly run !
Oh ! home of love and everlasting gladness !
　Oh ! crown unfading, and so early won !

Though tears will fall, we bless thee, O our
　　Father,
For the dear one for ever with the blest,
And wait the Easter dawn when Thou shalt
　　gather
Thine own, long parted, to their endless rest.

Rev. Canon Baynes, M.A.

'I would not live alway.'—*Job*, vii. 16.

THE Christian would not live always, because
he prefers perfect light to comparative darkness;
he prefers perfect and heavenly purity to partial
sanctification; immortal strength to earthly weakness; an endless peace and untroubled serenity
to agitations and storms; the blessed communion of the glorified to the society of the imperfect; the triumph of victory to the perils of
warfare.

Rev. John W. Hawtrey.

'*Their* angels.'—*St. Matt.* xviii. 10.

. . . . I THINK that we have rational grounds,
through '*comfort of the Scriptures*,' for hoping, if
not believing, that the beloved ones who have
gone from us do still remember us, and are still
interested in us. There is no sanction in Scripture for the idea that they *see* us. But that they
hear of us may be fairly inferred from our Lord's
words, which tell us that angels are employed
in bearing the tidings of a sinner's repenting
from Earth to Heaven, and that the result of
such information is joy to the pure spirits there.
A channel of communication is, therefore, open
between this world and the world of spirits—a
royal avenue, traversed by celestial messengers
who carry the tidings of every fresh triumph of
the Cross on earth to the resting souls in Paradise. Let no one say that this is useless specu-
lation. The issues of such a belief are strictly
practical. Our too eager desires for the things

of this world are thereby flattened, for we perceive that no record of the things that perish finds
its way along that heavenly road, while our desires after spiritual things are quickened and
stimulated by the thought that the knowledge of
our growth and progress in holiness is com-
municated to our departed friends, causing a new
thrill of happiness to their pure souls.

Oh, thought of deepest sweetness, that those
beloved ones who have left us, and whom our
hearts follow with yearning love, are still interested in us—nay, are *more* interested than they
could ever be on earth in each step of our
spiritual life ! Oh, thought of wondrous power,
too, that they are made acquainted with our
victories over sin and self ! Shall not this in-
spire us with a holy emulation to use all diligence in the 'way everlasting,' when we reflect
that, in proportion as our own souls grow and increase in the love of God our Saviour, so the
happiness of our absent ones is deepened and
intensified ? And this with no admixture of
anxiety or fear on their part ; for, seeing 'the

end of the Lord' as they now do, they can trust
Him for us, knowing that He is as able and
willing to save us as He was to save them.

May we not thus believe in the Communion
of Saints?

THE path of sorrow, and that path alone,
Leads to the land where sorrow is unknown;
No traveller ever reached that blest abode
Who found not thorns and briers on his road:
For He, who knew what human hearts would
      prove,
How slow to learn the dictates of His love,
That, hard by nature and of stubborn will,
A life of ease would make them harder still;
In pity to the souls His grace designed
To rescue from the ruins of mankind,
Called for a cloud to darken all their years,
And said, 'Go, spend them in the vale of tears.'

                            COWPER.

. . . . THERE are some who doubt whether heaven itself will renew their friendship. To scatter such a distressing apprehension, let the following reasons for expecting your friendship to revive again in heaven be attended to : You cannot think that the knowledge of glorified saints shall be more imperfect than their knowledge was while they were upon earth. We shall know much *more*, not *less*, than before. Heaven exceeds earth in knowledge as it does in joy. The angels in heaven have now a distinct knowledge of the least believer on earth, and rejoice in their conversion, and are styled by Christ 'their angels.' Therefore, when we shall be equal to the angels, we shall certainly know our nearest friends who will have their share with us in that glory. And though God be all in all in heaven, yet we shall there not only know, but love and rejoice in, our fellow-creatures. For Christ, in His glorified human nature, will be known and loved by all His members, without any diminution of the

glory of His divine nature. The future trium-
phant state of the Church is often described in
Scripture as a Kingdom, the City of God, the
New Jerusalem, each of which implies a society.
The people of God are to come from the east
and west, and sit down with Abraham, Isaac,
and Jacob in the kingdom of heaven ; and therefore they shall not only know those great
patriarchs, but shall take delight in their presence and converse. Love is a grace that never
faileth.

BAXTER.

Converse with God in Solitude.

THOUGH then thy cheek with deathless bloom
　　be sheen,
And rays of splendour wreathe thy sunlit brow,
That change I deem shall sever not between
Thee and thy former self, nor disallow
That love-tried eyes discern thee through the
　　screen
Of glory then, as of corruption now.

ANON.

*   *   *   *   *

THERE, meeting, who can guess the gleam
    Of rapture that will rise,
When we the light of that fair realm
    See in each other's eyes?

Oh deep, unspeakable repose,
    Of knowing that, for aye,
All that disturbed and hindered love
    Has wholly passed away!

Sin, sickness, sorrow, chills of age,
    And pangs of mortal fear,
Can never reach the land where Christ
    Has wiped away each tear.

For Death hath no dominion there,
    Where Sin has never trod,
But souls transfigured live and love
    Within the Life of God.

Then fear we not to trust His Word,
  And cherish Love's increase ;
Since e'en its sharpest throes must pass
  Into Eternal Peace.

C. NOEL.

. . . . . THIS trial may cast a shadow over your coming life. Be it so. Happy and blessed are they who count themselves pilgrims and sorrowing ones here ; so much the more keeping their eye fixed on the far-off land, where tears shall trickle down no more.

And while you are now shedding tears in desolation of spirit, your lost one lives calmly on, in the presence of his Redeemer, unspeakably fulfilled with His grace and heavenly benediction, so that you cannot go about your daily duties without a secret ascription of praise to Him who has so soon accomplished in that precious child the good pleasure of His will. Think of your child's enduring blessedness.

A. M. MAINGAY.

'Ye have need of patience.'—*Heb.* x. 36.

WHAT we want, then, is patience to endure. And this faith brings, for patience meekly endures that which faith pronounces to be just and true. Faith also whispers the promise of God, that there shall be an after-time to our sorrow, an after-taste of heavenly things. Ask of God this twin grace of faith and patience, suffering believer, and take thy burden cheerfully. Now it has a rough outside, but soon the heavy folds shall fall off under the warmth of God's love, and thou shalt find that what was so unpalatable before was but the wrapping of God's sweetmeats. A treasure shall then be revealed to thee which thy grief did but enfold to keep secure from harm and loss—a treasure of light, of love, of joy, and rest—the Spirit's cluster of the fruits of righteousness. O eternal God, Father of all mercies, God of all comfort, look upon us in all time of our tribulation,

and take away from our hearts all rebellious
strivings against Thy holy will! Increase our
faith and confirm our patience, and make us to
rest in Him who calls all weary ones to Himself; who Himself bare our sins and carried
our sorrows, even Jesus Christ the Son of Thy
love—the Anchor of our hope—the Author and
Finisher of our faith. Amen.

DAY after day we think what she is doing,
    In the bright realm of air;
Year after year her gentle steps pursuing,
    Behold her grown more fair.
Thus do we walk with her, and keep unbroken
    The bond that Nature gives,
Thinking that our remembrance unspoken
    May reach her where she lives.

                                LONGFELLOW.

THE CHAMBER OF PEACE.

'The Pilgrim they laid in a large upper chamber facing
the sun-rising. The name of the chamber was Peace.'—
Pilgrim's Progress.

AFTER the burden and heat of the day,
 The starry calm of night;
After the rough and toilsome way,
 A sleep in the robe of white.

O blessèd Pilgrim ! we see thy face
 As an angel's face might seem,
For lying pale in that shadowy place
 Thou dreamest a golden dream.

The stars are watching the sleeping saint,
 And lighting the sleeping brow,
But the light of the stars is cold and faint
 To the glory he dreameth now.

For the things that are hid from waking eyes
 Shine clear to the veilèd sight;
From the chamber dim where the pilgrim lies
 We can watch the fountains of light.

The journey is over, the fight is fought,
  He hath seen the Home of his love,
And the smile on the dreamer's face is caught
  From the land of smiles above.

Thou hast another chamber, dear Lord,
  The secret place of peace,
Where Thy precious ones are safely stored
  When their weary wanderings cease.

After the burden and heat of the day,
  The starry calm of night;
After the rough and toilsome way,
  A sleep in the robe of white.

The sacred chamber is still and wide,
  You listen in vain for a breath;
And pale lie the sleepers side by side,
  In the cold moonlight of death.

No sighs are heard in the shadowy place,
  No voices of them that weep;
They have fought the fight and finished the race:
  God giveth them rest in sleep.

E

Oh ! sweet is the slumber wherewith the King
　　Hath caused the weary to rest !
For sleeping they hear the angels sing,
　　They lean on the Master's breast.

And sweet is the chamber, silent and wide,
　　Where lingers the holy smile
Of a wayfaring Man, who turned aside
　　To rest, long ago, for a while.

He had suffered a sorrow which none may tell,
　　He had purchased a gift unpriced ;
When His work was over, the moonlight fell
　　On the sleeping face of Christ—

The face of a victor dead and crowned,
　　With a smile divinely fair ;
The saints and martyrs sleeping around
　　Were stirred as *He* entered there.*

His very name is as ointment poured
　　On the moonlight pale to-night ;
And the chamber is sweet to Thy servants, Lord,
　　For the scent of Thy raiment white.

　　　　* Matt. xxvii. 52.

The silent chamber faceth the east,
   Faceth the dawn of day,
And the shining feet of our great High Priest
   Shall break through the shadows grey.

The golden dawn of the day of God
   Shall smite on the sealèd eyes;
The trumpet's sound shall thunder around,
   The dreamers shall wake and rise.

The night is over, the sleep is slept,
   They are called from their shadowy place;
The pilgrims stand in the glorious land,
   And gaze on their Master's face.

                                B. M.

NOTHING is lost that is loved in God, since in
   Him all things are saved to us.

                         S. BERNARD.

Now, while they were thus drawing towards the gate, behold, a company of the heavenly host came out to meet them; to whom it was said by the other two shining ones, 'These are the men that have loved our Lord when they were in the world, and that have left all for His Holy Name; and He hath sent us to fetch them, and we have brought them thus far on their desired journey, that they may go in and look their Redeemer in the face with joy.'

. . . . And now were these two men, as it were, in heaven before they came at it, being swallowed up with a sight of angels, and with hearing their melodious notes. . . . . But, above all, the warm and joyful thoughts that they had about their own dwelling there with such company, and that for ever and ever. Oh! by what tongue or pen can their glorious joy be expressed? . . . . Now, just as the gates were opened to let in the men, I looked in after

them; and behold, the City shone like the sun,
the streets also were paved with gold, and in
them walked many men with crowns on their
heads, palms in their hands, and golden harps to
sing praises withal. . . . . And, after that, they
shut up the gates; which, when I had seen, I
wished myself amongst them.

Pilgrim's Progress.

FAIN would I catch a hymn of love
From the angel-harps which ring above,
And sing it as my parting breath
Quivered and expired in death ;
So that those on earth might hear
The harp-notes of another sphere,
And mark, when nature faints and dies,
What springs of heavenly life arise,
And gather from the death they view
A ray of hope to light them through,
When they should be departing too.

EDMESTON.

IN MEMORIAM.

THE REV. ERNEST WIGRAM,

Entered into rest September 6th, 1876.

GONE ! O'er this world's waves no longer
Is thy tender vessel borne ;
Gone from where the holiest efforts
Only meet the bitterest scorn ;

Gone from life's unceasing struggle,
From that keen and Cross-led fight,
Where the serried ranks of Jesus
Serve beneath His banner bright ;

Gone from work for His dear glory,
From the souls thou lov'dst to bless,
From the toil so free for others,
In thy sweet unselfishness ;

Gone from standing at His altar
In thy vesture snowy white ;
Gone from all the priestly service
Laid before Him day and night ;

Gone, through pain and patient suffering,
  By the path of woe He trod ;
Gone to rest on Jesu's bosom
  In the Paradise of God ;

Gone to serve in higher worship,
  In a brighter vestment clad,
Where the Beatific Vision
  Makes the hosts of angels glad.

But the labour wrought so nobly,
  And the life laid down for Christ,
Evermore shall breathe a fragrance
  Which the Church shall hold unpriced.

And thy light can ne'er burn lower,
  Though men's thoughts of thee may cease ;
Therefore, in those arms so loving,
  Now and ever ' Rest in peace.'

JOHN FABER SCHOLFIELD.

Whitby, 11*th Sept.* 1876.

IN the first anguish of bereavement we are conscious of a pressure still heavier than that of
sorrow : it is the burden of *love*. Indeed, the
measure of our love is the measure of our
sorrow ; as they rightly judged who said, when
Jesus wept at the grave of Lazarus, 'Behold
how He loved him !

In the texture of our grief there is a wondrous
blending of feelings, but the warp and woof of
it is *love :* love, in its truest, keenest, and fullest
exercise : love, in a sense of drawing towards
the object beloved, and with a desire of union
such as we have never realised before.

'Why did we not love like this,' our heart
cries out, 'when our dear one was with us?'
Alas! it is not possible. It is death alone
that has power to unlock the treasure and reveal
the wealth of human love. This is touchingly
expressed by Lord Houghton in the following
lines :—

'The rain that falls upon the height,
Too gently to be called delight,
In the dark valley reappears
As a wild cataract of tears;
And love, in life, shall strive to see
Sometimes what love in death would be.'

How shall we bear this burden of yearning love? There is only one way. Let us take it to the great Burden-bearer, and ask Him to show us God's meaning in it. By the dim foreshadowing of the finite He will lead us to grasp the idea of the Infinite, and to believe in the existence of a Divine Love, the patience, and tenderness, and self-sacrifice of which is but feebly interpreted by the strongest human affection.

O suffering human heart, thou shalt yet bless the burden of love which threatens to overwhelm thee now, when it helps thee to apprehend and receive that amazing Love of Christ, which, stronger than death, even the death of the Cross, has waited for long years, though disregarded and unrequited by thee, to bless thee through union and communion with Itself.

Thus it is that by the analogies of earth we
rise into the mystery of Heaven. Thus do the
earthly ties of our human affections become
stepping-stones over the troubled waters of Self,
to the great shore of Eternal Love and Rest.

O HAUNTED soul,
Down whose dim corridors for ever roll
The voices of the dead—whose holy ground
Re-echoes, at the midnight hour, with sound
Of feet that long ago were laid to rest,
Yet trouble thee for ever. Lo ! a Guest
Is waiting at thy gate ; and unto Him
Thou shalt bemoan thy dead, and He will take
Sweet words and comfort thee. Thine eyes are
        dim,
But stretch thine hands to Him : He will not
        break
The bruisèd reed.

                              B. M.

THOU wert the first of all I knew
　　To pass unto the dead,
And Paradise hath seemed more true,
And come down closer to my view,
　　Since there thy presence fled.

The whispers of thy gentle soul
　　At silent, lowly hours,
Like some sweet saint-bell's distant toll,
Come o'er the waters as they roll
　　Betwixt thy world and ours.

Oh ! still my spirit clings to thee,
　　And feels thee at my side,
Like a green ivy when the tree
Its shoots have clasped so lovingly
　　Within its arms hath died.

REV. T. WHYTEHEAD.

THE DEATH OF THE CHRISTIAN.

THE Apostle slept—a light shone in the prison,
  An angel touched his side ;
' Arise,' he said, and quickly hath he risen,
  His fettered arms untied.

The watchers saw no light at midnight gleaming,
  They heard no sound of feet ;
The gates fly open, and the saint, still dreaming,
  Stands free upon the street.

So, when the Christian's eyelid droops and closes,
  In Nature's parting strife,
A friendly angel stands where he reposes,
  To wake him up to life.

He gives a gentle blow, and so releases
  The spirit from its clay ;
From sins, temptations, and from life's distresses,
  He bids it come away.

It rises up, and from its darksome mansion
   It takes its silent flight,
And feels its freedom in the large expansion
   Of heavenly air and light.

Behind, it hears Time's iron gates close faintly :
   It now is far from them ;
For it has reached the City of the Saintly,
   The New Jerusalem.

A voice is heard on earth of kinsfolk weeping
   The loss of one they love,
But he is gone where the redeemed are keeping
   A Festival above.

The mourners throng the way, and from the steeple
   The funeral bell tolls slow,
But on the golden streets the holy people
   Are passing to and fro.

And saying as they meet, 'Rejoice ! another,
   Long waited for, is come.'
The Saviour's heart is glad, a younger brother
   Hath reached the Father's Home.

                    REV. J. D. BURNS, M.A.

. . . . 'TRULY, Maurice, you are a happy man. It is good, indeed, to sow in tears for the gain of such reaping. You must feel, too, that it is another token of God's lovingkindness that the child you so much loved was made by Him the means of bringing you to Himself.'

'They say that in some countries the shepherd takes the lamb from its mother and carries it in her sight up the mountains, in order to induce the sheep to follow. I have seen it in a picture, and I have thought that perhaps it is for the same reason that God takes so many little children unto Himself.'

'You are right, indeed. It is that thought which has put to silence that faithless *why* which at first troubled me so much. "Why," I said, "does God give me so much power to love if it is to be only the channel of suffering?" Now I see that if I had not loved I had not suffered, and if I had not suffered I should never have sought Him who receiveth sinners. It is all clear now why little Jeanie was sent into the world. Her life and death had God's own meaning in them, and I shall read it more clearly still when we meet before the throne of God and of the Lamb.'

'You have the golden key to the mystery of human pain, Maurice. Good were it if all sorrowing parents saw their losses in this light. To have a child in heaven, and yet to remain far from God, is the saddest of all things; for God must surely intend that sainted children in heaven should make holy parents on earth. It is a sweet and solemn thought, and one full of reality, that to this end He sends little children into this world of sin and sorrow, as He sent angels of old with messages of mercy to the families of men.'

From *The Man at the Helm.*

. . . . JESUS CHRIST weeps with you, but He bids you smile through your tears. Think of a child in heaven with Christ, freed at once from the guilt of sin, and from a deceitful and desperately wicked heart with which it came into the world, and which might have manifested itself in entire and perpetual departure from the Lord. Think of the negative ; think of the positive. I condole with you, yet I congratulate with you —indeed, from my heart I do. Your sorrow time will soothe ; your joy in this instance will increase more and more. To have a child with the Lord ! Think of that ! a lovely plant in the Garden of Paradise, and the fruit of the Spirit, love, and joy, and peace, in ever-ripening clusters. God comfort you !

REV. THOMAS BROCK.

LOVE's very grief is gain ;
Thereby earth holier grows and heaven is nigher ;
Souls that their idols may not here detain,
    Will follow and aspire.

Potent is sorrow's breath
To quench wrath's fever ; and the hungry will
That clutches fame looks in the face of death,
    And the wild mien is still.

No paths of sense may wile
The yearning heart.   It asks not if the road
Have bays to crown or odours to beguile,
    But—*does it lead to God?*

Love, purity, repose,
Faith cherished, duty done, and wrong forgiven ;
Be these the garland and the staff of those
    Who have a child in heaven.

                   ANON.

'For I know their sorrows.'—*Exod.* iii. 7.

WHEN across the heart deep waves of sorrow
  Break as on a dry and barren shore;
When hope glistens with no bright to-morrow,
  And the storm seems sweeping evermore;

When the cup of every earthly gladness
  Bears no taste of the life-giving stream,
And high hopes, as though to mock our sadness,
  Fade and die as in some fitful dream;

Who shall hush the weary spirit's chiding?
  Who the aching void shall fill?
Who shall whisper of a peace abiding,
  And each surging billow calmly still?

Only He whose wounded heart was broken
  With the bitter cross and thorny crown,
Whose dear love glad words of joy had spoken,
  Who His life for us laid meekly down.

Blessed Healer! all our burdens lighten,
  Give us peace—Thine own sweet peace—we
    pray ;   .
Keep us near Thee till the morn shall brighten,
  And all mists and shadows flee away !

REV. CANON BAYNES.

LOVE thou thy sorrow !   Grief shall bring
  Its own excuse in after years :
The Rainbow—see how fair a thing
  God hath built up from tears !

ANON.

. . . . FOR He Who has willingly borne the
sins of the world—so revolting a burden to one
Who was Purity itself—can and will bear the
sorrows of His children.

'And being in an agony He prayed more earnestly, and
His sweat was as it were great drops of blood falling
down to the ground.'—*St. Luke*, xxii. 44.

Do you not think that the chief end God has
in sending us sorrow is, to arrest our minds and
fix our attention upon the sorrows of Christ?
It must be so, because, when our own hearts are
bleeding, we find that the Cross of Jesus is our
only true comfort and our only true strength.
When we have truly looked upon Him Whom
our sins have pierced and begun to mourn for
Him, we learn to look less at our own grief,
and to mourn less for ourselves. We all pro-
fess to believe in the mysterious anguish of the
'Passion,' but we study it very little in the time
of our prosperity. When tribulation comes,
there is a silence in our soul; then we turn
aside to see this great sight. We see then that
there must be wonderful meaning in that wonderful sorrow, and now that our own hearts are

tasting pain we can better approach the grief
that bowed the head of our Elder Brother,
Christ. We see the reality of sin in the costly
price of its redemption, and all hard thoughts
of God are condemned within us; we cease to
demand of life happiness as a right, and we
discern presently, in the light of God's light,
that they are most blessed who mourn. The
Valley of Tears, we perceive, leads to the
Mountain of Consolation. We are, therefore,
not surprised or affrighted when tribulation
comes. Yea, God gives us grace in the aftertime
to rejoice in that sorrow which is 'conforming us
to the Image of the Son.' Did the Saviour drink
so deeply of the cup of pain for us? How then
shall we doubt His love or willingness to save
us from all suffering that is not absolutely needful
for us? Shall we not be ready to take any cup
from the 'Hand that was pierced to give those
beloved ones who have gone before their Paradise of rest and joy?' So be it Lord. Amen.

. . . . You have lost a child : nay, she is not lost to you—she is found to Christ. She is not sent away, but only sent before—like unto a star, which, going out of sight, doth not die and vanish, but shineth in another hemisphere. You see her not, yet she doth shine in another country. If her glass was but a short hour, what she wanteth of time that she hath gotten of eternity; and you have to rejoice that you have now some treasure laid up in heaven.

*　　*　　*　　*　　*

She is but gone an hour or two sooner to bed, as children use to do, and we are undressing to follow. And the more we put off the love of this present world, and all things superfluous beforehand, we shall have the less to do when we lie down.

ARCHBISHOP LEIGHTON.

'IT IS WELL!'

SINCE thy Father's arm sustains thee,
      Peaceful be;
When a chastening hand restrains thee,
      It is He.
Know His love, in full completeness,
Fills the measure of thy weakness:
  If He wound thy spirit sore,
      Trust Him more.

Without murmur, uncomplaining,
      In His hand
Lay whatever things thou canst not
      Understand.
Though the world the folly spurneth,
From thy faith in pity turneth,
  Peace thy inmost soul shall fill,
      Lying still.

Like an infant, if thou thinkest
  Thou canst stand,
Childlike proudly pushing back
  The offered hand,
Courage soon is changed to fear,
Strength doth feebleness appear,—
 In His love if thou abide,
  He will guide.

Fearest sometimes that thy Father
  Hath forgot?
When the clouds around thee gather,
  Doubt Him not.
Always hath the daylight broken,
Always hath He comfort spoken;
 Better hath He been for years,
  Than thy fears.

Therefore, whatsoe'er betideth
  Night or day,
Know His love for thee provideth
  Good alway.

Crown of sorrow gladly take,
Grateful wear it for His sake,
  Sweetly bending to His will,
    Lying still.

To His own thy Saviour giveth
    Daily strength ;
To each troubled soul that liveth,
    Peace at length.
Weakest lambs have largest share
Of the tender Shepherd's care ;
  Ask Him not, then, 'When,' or 'How,'
    Only bow.

               PAUL GERHARDT.

'OH! if you knew the joy of an *accepted* sorrow !'

               MADAME GUYON.

'Search me, O Lord, and try me, and lead me in the way everlasting.'—*Ps.* cxxxix. 23.

WHEN Thought is doing her work in the quiet hours of our grief, let us press out the full blessing that is found in the knowledge that the Holy Spirit, the 'Comforter,' is the Spirit of Truth. It implies, not only that the measure of our light will be the measure of our consolation, which is a most precious truth, but that when God comforts us it must be only in the way of *truth*. In this way lies much that is painful, but it is the right way, because it is the 'way everlasting.' In the hour of affliction the Spirit of Truth is as the candle of the Lord, searching the inmost recesses of our sinful hearts. Only those who have been much alone with God, either through bodily sickness or mental suffering, know what that searching is. When the closed shutters of our self-righteousness are taken down, the day-light of truth reveals to us the 'hidden things

of darkness.' What unexpected sins we then
discover, perhaps, for the first time! What
hard thoughts of God! what rebellious strivings .
against His holy will! what folly in our so-called
wisdom! what selfishness in our so-called gene-
rosity! what evil habits of thought and action
in our childhood, our youth, and our riper years!
When in God's light we thus see light, we should
indeed be overwhelmed by despair if it were not
for the cleansing blood of Him upon whom 'our
iniquities were laid,' and who only shows us our
sin that He may deliver us from it and lead us
in 'the way everlasting.' 'If, indeed,' says a
good man, 'God were known to us only as a
Reprover, we might be justified in shrinking
from closer contact with Him; if the light
which is so painful when it breaks in upon
our darkness sought entrance only to condemn,
then we might close our eyes: but there is *forgiveness* with our God that He may be feared,
and with Him there is plenteous redemption.'

O God the Holy Ghost, give unto me, I
pray Thee, uprightness of desire to bring myself

under Thy searching eye. Make me willing
that Thou shouldest carry Thy candle into
the dark recesses of my heart. Let me be
not afraid to place myself in Thy hands.
Grant that in looking back upon a time of
searching I may never fear a repetition of it,
but give me grace always to yield myself un-
reservedly to Thy will, and to Thy love. Show
me what Thou Thyself seest in me, that I may
be saved from myself.

So search me, O God of Truth; so try me,
O Blessed Comforter, and lead me in the way
everlasting; for Jesu's sake. Amen.

GOD alone
Instructeth how to mourn. He doth not trust
This higher lesson to a voice or hand
Subordinate. Behold! *He* cometh forth!
O sweet disciple, bow thyself to learn
    The alphabet of tears.

SIGOURNEY.

. . . . . SYMPATHY implies suffering—suffering
along with another, and on account of that
other's sufferings. It is that fellow-feeling of
sorrow which constrains us to weep with them
that weep. It is sympathy which St. Paul
enjoins when he bids us ' remember them that
are in bonds, *as bound with them* ' (Heb. xiii. 3).
Such, at least, is the full meaning of the term ;
but in common speech it is often used to
designate something less than this. Archbishop
Trench tells us that certain words have a constant tendency to deteriorate in value. Man,
anxious to hide the poverty of his feelings under
the grandeur of his expressions, is tempted to
employ a strong word in order to represent a
very meagre thing, until, through the continuance of this exaggeration, the word itself loses
its first meaning, and comes to stand only for
what it is really worth. Sympathy is one of

such words. But when we speak of the sympathy of Jesus, we need to subtract no discount
from the full value of the term. He, and He
alone, fills up to its widest stretch of meaning all
that it implies ; and far, far more. Oh, what a
blessed resting-place for the faith of the tried
believer ! We must on no account, then, dis-
honour Christ's sympathy by comparing it with
our own or with our fellows'; for as the heavens
are higher than the earth, so are His thoughts
higher than our thoughts. Moreover, our sympathy, alas ! meagre as it is, is foolish at the
best, and sadly misplaced. When we weep
with others, our tears are often wasted on such
outside circumstances of the sorrow as are not
really worth our faintest sigh. But the sympathy of Jesus is as perfect in its wisdom as it
is in its tenderness. It is worthy of Him who
is 'the power of God and the wisdom of God.'
So then, my suffering brother, will you, for your
comfort and your profit, think less upon the
circumstances of your sorrow, and more upon
the love that sends it ? Will you lift your

weeping eyes from off the heavy hand that
presses you, and look rather into the gracious
Face, so radiant with sympathising love?   Oh!
there is a heaven of comfort for you—humbling,
sanctifying comfort—in the holy tenderness of
those meek yet piercing eyes of flame, whose
glance so wounds and yet so heals—yea, wounds
still more with the glance that heals!

J. D.

Oh! think awhile,
It matters little at what hour o' the day
The righteous fall asleep.   Death cannot come
To him untimely who is fit to die.
The less of this cold world—the more of Heaven;
The briefer life—the earlier immortality.

MILMAN.

HYMN.

When musing Sorrow weeps the past,
   And mourns the present pain,
'Tis sweet to think of peace at last,
   And feel that death is gain.

'Tis not that murmuring thoughts arise,
   And dread a Father's will;
'Tis not that meek submission flies,
   And would not suffer still ;

It is that Heaven-born Faith surveys
   The path that leads to light,
And longs her eagle plumes to raise,
   And lose herself in flight.

It is that hope with ardour glows
   To see *Him* face to face,
Whose dying love no language knows
   Sufficient art to trace.

It is that harassed conscience feels
    The pangs of struggling sin,
And sees, though far, the hand that heals,
    And ends the strife within.

Oh, let me wing hallowèd strife
    From earth-born woe and care,
And soar above these clouds of night
    My Saviour's bliss to share.

HON. AND REV. GERALD NOEL.

DEATH doth lurk always in life's delicious cup,—
The mulberry-leaf must bear the biting of a
        worm,
That so it may be raised to wear its silken form.

RUCKERT.

G

IN MEMORIAM: E. S.

ONCE the sentence justly sounded,
   ' Thou shalt die !' in accents dread,
To the erring sheep who wandered,
   In forbidden paths to tread.
But how awfully it lighted
   On the Saviour's sinless head !

And since He endured that anguish,
   Bore those sorrows deep and vast,
For His people death is altered,
   All its bitterness is past.
As they journey where He leads them,
   'Tis a step, and that the last.

So, from time to time the Master
   Calleth home His servants still,
One by one, the many mansions
   In His Father's house to fill.
Shall we dare His love to question,
   Or dispute His sovereign will?

Go in peace, belovèd brother!
  At the call of Jesus go,
To behold Him in His beauty,
  All His love and grace to know.
Thou departest—we must linger
  In the land of sin and woe.

Rest in peace! the rest is pleasant,
  When our toil and strife are o'er;
All the sweeter for the conflict,
  Or the weariness before.
Thou hast laboured long and nobly,
  Thou shalt rest for evermore.

While thy memory we cherish,
  Ever honoured, ever dear,
Till we meet again, when Jesus
  Shall have banished every tear,
And, with rapture re-united,
  All thy tale of glory hear.

ANON.

'For we have not an high priest which cannot be touched
with the feeling of our infirmities ; but was in all points
tempted like as we are, yet without sin.'—*Heb.* iv. 15.

JESUS ! my sorrow lies too deep
    For human ministry ;
It knows not how to tell itself
    To any but to Thee.

Thou dost remember still, amid
    The glories of God's throne,
The sorrows of mortality,
    For they were once Thine own.

Yes ! for as if Thou wouldst be God,
    E'en in Thy misery,
There's been no sorrow but Thine own
    Untouched by sympathy.

Jesus ! my fainting spirit brings
    Its fearfulness to Thee;
Thine eye, at least, can penetrate
    The clouded mystery.

It is enough, my precious Lord,
    Thy tender sympathy !
There is no sorrow e'er so deep
    But I may bring to Thee.

HE who loved her best
Did what was best, and we that wept His will
Yet praise Him; praise Him for the treasure
    lent,—
For that sweet angel visit, which, unawares,
We entertained; for that dear memory,
Which makes the past of those five winged
    months
An Eden of remembrance : more than all,
We now have learnt to praise Him, that again
Into His blessed keeping, undefiled,
He took her back to meet us at ' that day.'

              S. J. STONE.
        From *Our Lambs in the Fold above.*

'O LORD, MY STRENGTH!'

MAN in his weakness needs a stronger stay
    Than fellow-men, the holiest and the best;
And yet we turn to them from day to day,
    As if in them our spirits could find rest.

Gently untwine our childish hands that cling
    To such inadequate supports as these,
And shelter us beneath Thy heavenly wing
    Till we have learned to walk alone with ease.

Help us, O Lord, with patient love, to bear
    Each other's faults, to suffer with true meek-
       ness;
Help us each other's joys and griefs to share,
    But let us turn to Thee alone in weakness.

From *The Dove on the Cross.*

. . . . WHEN —— was dying, he said, 'Two
months ago, when I knew this sickness was unto
death, I asked Jesus to reveal Himself to me in
increased loveliness and nearness. He did so;
and now His love, His beauty, His perfection,
fill my heart and vision.' When I spoke of
his being a little better he said, 'All that is no
pleasure to me. My precious Lord Jesus! Thou
knowest how fully I can say, "To depart and be
with Thee is far better." They come and talk
to me of a crown of glory—I bid them cease;
of the glories of Heaven—I bid them stop. I
am not wanting crowns; I have Himself, *Himself!* I am going to be with Himself—with the
Man of Sychar, with Him who stayed to call
Zaccheus, with the Man of the eighth of John,
with the Man who hung upon the cross, with
the Man who died! Oh! to be with Him
before the glories, the crowns, and the king-
doms appear—it is wonderful! With the Man
of Sychar *alone*, the Man at the gate of Nain—
with Him for ever!' From *A Living Epistle.*

THEN, when my race on earth is run,
My day of work and waiting done,
And I, with tottering footsteps, wend
Nearer to what men call 'my end,'
And they in whom life's tide is high
With pitying whisper pass me by—
I ask no pity for my fate,
Nay, rather, friends, congratulate!
For Home is near! and it is late!
And when beneath the church's shade
My lifeless body hath been laid,
With such sweet words of prayer and praise
As men round Christian death-beds raise;
Let none, as for some lost one, weep—
'He giveth His belovèd sleep.'
Let no one think of me with pain,
'To live is Christ, to die is gain.'
Let it be neither thought nor said,
'Alas, poor fellow! he is dead!'
He wants not pity, nor is poor,
Nor dead, whose life and joy are sure!

Say, rather, 'Thank God, he at last
Is safe, all sins and sorrows past.
"Gone home!" that is the only word
That should from Christian lips be heard—
"No more with weary steps to roam
Earth's wilderness—gone home! gone home!"'

REV. DR. MONSELL.
From *Near Home at Last.*

I BLESS Thee for the quiet rest
  Thy servant taketh now;
I bless Thee for his blessedness,
  And for his crownèd brow.
For every weary step he took
  In faithful following Thee,
And for the good fight foughten well,
  And closed right valiantly.

BISHOP SHIRLEY.

AN old writer says, 'It matters not at which of the thousand doors of death we go out, while we know that He who hath the keys of death is with us in the passage to conduct us safely to the invisible world.' Still we have reason to bless God with exceeding gratitude when, in His own appointed time, He delivers us from bodily pain, and grants to us peacefully to fall asleep in Him. Who is there among us that has not brought away from some grave the rich legacy of the holy example of a happy death-bed—the memory, perchance, of a beloved parent? We remember the words of faith and love which came from the lips upon which the shadows of death were deepening. We can still see the glow of celestial light which irradiated the pale features. At such times we need no argument to convince us of the solemn realities of the unseen world. We see that the hour of nature's sorest need is the hour of God's richest consolation, for we perceive that the departing soul as it enters the dark valley begins to see

something beyond, which is hidden from our
eyes, and in that foretaste of its celestial
triumph it conquers death, and finds 'abundant
entrance' into the kingdom. Are not such
influences felt all the more in the example of
aged Christians? 'As ripe fruit is sweeter than
green fruit,' says one, 'so is age sweeter than
youth: provided the youth were grafted into
Christ. As harvest-time is brighter than seed-
time, so is age brighter than youth: that is, if
youth were a seed-time for good. As the com-
pletion of a work is more glorious than the
beginning, so age is more glorious than youth:
that is, if the foundation of the work of God
were laid in youth. As sailing into port is a
happier thing than the voyage, so is age happier
than youth: that is, when the voyage from youth
is made with Christ at the helm.' Thus it is
fulfilled, that 'at evening time it shall be light;'
for though the shadows of evening are stretched
out, and the day of this mortal life goeth away,
the 'path of the just is as the shining light, that
shineth more and more unto the perfect day.'

He said,
In faltering accents, to the weeping train,
'Why mourn ye that our aged friend is dead?
Ye are not sad to see the gathered grain,
Nor when the mellow fruit the orchards cast,
Nor when the yellow woods shake down their
    ripened mast.

Ye sigh not when the sun, his course fulfilled—
    His glorious course, rejoicing earth and sky—
In the soft evening, when the winds are stilled,
    Sinks where the islands of refreshment lie,
And leaves the smile of his departure spread
O'er the warm-coloured heaven and ruddy
    mountain head.

Why weep ye, then, for him, who, having run
    The bound of man's appointed years, at last,
God's promises fulfilled, life's labours done,
    Serenely to his final rest has passed;
While the soft memory of his virtues yet
Lingers like twilight hues when the bright sun
    is set?'

BRYANT.

How fair has the day been ! how bright was the
    sun,
How lovely and joyful the course that he ran !
Though he rose in a mist, when his race he
    began,
  And there followed some droppings of rain.
But now, as the traveller comes to the west,
His rays are all gold and his beauties are best ;
He paints the sky gay as he sinks to his rest,
  And foretells a bright rising again.

And such the believer ! his course he begins,
Like the sun in a mist, when he mourns for his
    sins,
And melts into tears; then he breaks out and
    shines,
  And travels his heavenly way.
But when he comes nearer to finish his race,
Like a bright setting sun he looks richer in
    grace,
And gives a sure hope, at the end of his days,
  Of rising in brighter array.
                ISAAC WATTS.

. . . . EARTHLY affections are elevated by bereavement. God would have us fix our love
where He has deposited one of our treasures.
The following illustration will bring home this
truth: ' I was riding,' says a clergyman of New
York, ' on the western shore of the Hudson,
and, passing a substantial mansion, I observed
carriages standing around the entrance, and a
hearse, that plainly indicated the occasion of
the gathering. It was something more than
curiosity—it was the dictate of natural sympathy that induced me to stop and mingle
with the multitude. It was easy to learn
from the first whom I addressed that a young
man, the son of parents advanced in life, was
to be buried. The clergyman in attendance
was just closing his remarks when I stopped at
the door; and after a short but eloquent pause
in the services the afflicted father rose, and,
overcoming his emotion, spoke a few words

with the friends that surrounded him. He said: "A few months ago one of my sons removed to the other side of the river, and he resides on the shore in view of the spot where we are assembled. And now I find my thoughts are over there far more frequently than they were before. I had friends there whom 'I loved, and I had an interest in the people, but I had no son there; but since that child has been a resident beyond the river my heart is there often, and I love to be there. So it has been with me during the few days that have passed since this other son has crossed the river of death, and, as I trust, entered Heaven. My thoughts are often there now, True, I had friends there before—a father there —but I had no *child* there. Now, I have an interest in Heaven such as I never felt till one of my children went there to live !"'

REV. T. HATCHARD.
From *The Floweret Gathered.*

LET us put a right construction on all God's dealings with our souls, especially in our seasons of affliction. Let us not be hasty. Let us take God's work together, and not judge of it by parcels. It is, indeed, all wisdom and righteousness; but we shall best discern the beauty of it when we look on it in the frame, when it shall be fully completed and finished, and our eyes enlightened to take a fuller and clearer view of it than we can have here. Oh! what gratitude, what wonder, it will then command! We read of Joseph, hated and sold, and imprisoned, and all most unjustly; yet, because within a leaf or two we find him freed and exalted, and his brethren coming as supplicants to him, we are satisfied. But when we look on things which are for the present cloudy and dark, our short-sighted, hasty spirits cannot learn to wait a little till we see the other side, and what end the Lord makes.

LEIGHTON.

' And was gathered to his people.'—*Gen.* xxv. 8.

CHEERLESS, indeed, would be the thought as
we lay beloved relatives in the grave, ' I shall
see you no more for ever.' We cling to the
belief that there shall be renewed friendships,
undying restoration of earth's sweetest fellow-
ships. How comforting, especially, must this
expectation be to those who, like Abraham, are
' full of years '—the last of their generation ; the
friends of early life removed, the village or street
or city where they were born filled with new
and unrecognised faces, the lights in their own
homestead one by one extinguished, the trees of
the home forest one by one cut down, and the
gnarled trunks alone remaining ! How cheering
for them to think, when stretched on a death-
bed, that they are not so much going *from* home
as *to* home ; that if they wish to be '*gathered to
their people*' they must go to Heaven ! That

H

that ' dark valley ' from which they used, in the buoyant days of youth, to start as at something fearful, is really the avenue leading up to their Father's dwelling-place—the rendezvous of their kindred ! As they draw near they hear music and joy, and many a familiar voice exclaiming, 'This my parent, my brother, my son, was dead and is alive again ; he was lost and is found !'

REV. DR. MACDUFF.

THESE, in life's distant even,
Shall shine serenely bright,
As, in th' autumnal heaven,
Mild rainbow tints at night :
When the last shower is stealing down,
And, ere they sink to rest,
The sunbeams weave a parting crown
For some sweet woodland nest.

The promise of the morrow
  Is glorious on that eve,
Dear as the holy sorrow
  When good men cease to live;
When, brightening ere it die away,
  Mounts up their altar-flame,
Still tending with intenser ray
  To Heaven, whence first it came.

Say not it dies, that glory,
  'Tis caught unquenched on high;
Those saintlike brows so hoary
  Shall wear it in the sky.
No smile is like the smile of death,
  When, all good musings past,
Rise wafted with the parting breath
  The sweetest thought the last.

From *The Christian Year.*

'Then are they glad because they are at rest; and so He bringeth them unto the haven where they would be.'—*Ps.* cvii. 30.

I STOOD on the deep-blue ocean's shore,
And watched the wild sea-bird lave,
While murmuring low fell sweet on my ear
The flow of the passing wave.

When, dancing light in the morning bright,
A fair little bark came by;
Its tiny white sail so joyously shone
With a gleam from the sunny sky.

And I thought of youth, of its early morn,
Fresh launched on life's restless wave,
When each gale that blows with fresh odour is fraught
To the young heart so gladsome and brave.

That gleam vanished soon; the sky was o'ercast;
In terror the sail was furled;
I thought of the Christian mariner, tossed
On the waves of this troublesome world.

·On the rough billows' foam the little bark
  Was tossing from side to side ;
I marvelled it sank not, but One was there—
  Jesus, the Ruler and Guide.

No empty shells had the mariner sought
  From the barren and sandy ground,
Deep treasured within his bosom there lay
  The Pearl of great price he had found.

The darkness came on—the tempest rose high,
  And I heard the breakers roar ;
But the little vessel bore bravely on,
  Fast nearing a glorious shore.

The morning broke on that night of sorrow,
  A morning serene and still ;
I looked for the bark—it was safely moored
  In the haven under the hill.

The white sail was furled, the anchor dropped, ·
  The winds were hushed to a sleep,
And gently the bark wafted to and fro,
  On the face of the glassy deep.

Oh ! best the repose, eternal the peace,
Of the ransomed soul shall be ;
No ' toiling in rowing,' no fear of storm,
For ' *there shall be no more sea.*'

L. A. B.

' The God of Patience and Consolation.'—*Rom.* xv. 5.

LET us notice that Patience comes before Consolation. This touches a very common mistake made by sorrowing Christians. They are apt to think that God is not well pleased with them if they *continue* to sorrow, and so they make haste to be comforted; but it is not through comfort of the Scriptures. How often we hear change of air—change of scene—diversion of thought, pressed upon the mourner by mistaken ·advisers, who fall·into the error of placing consolation before patience !

But there is a spiritual order in God's purpose for us, and He makes no mistakes. When He sends us the 'bread of tears' let us not put it aside for the 'oil of joy,' but possess our souls in patience until He Himself shall wipe away those tears. His wisdom is equal to His love, and appoints the measure and continuance of our pain. Forget not, O sorrowing believer, that there is an evening as well as a morning in all God's works. Seek not to cloud the one by shadows of thy own creating, and still less to light up the other with the false glare of this world's comforts. Be patient until the coming of that day when the Lord shall be unto thee 'an everlasting light, and thy God thy glory.'

'OH ! there is never a sorrow of heart,
    That shall lack a timely end,
If but to God we turn and pray,
    And ask Him to be our friend.'

WORDSWORTH.

'Because I live, ye shall live also.'—*John*, xiv. 19.

Why march ye forth with hymn and chant,
Ye veteran soldiers jubilant,
As though ye went to lay to rest
Some warrior that had done his best?
  —Because we do but travel o'er
  The road the Victor trod before;
  Himself knows well the way we go:
  The Son of Man is Lord also
    Of the grave-path.

Commit your loved one to the surge
Without a wail, without a dirge?
To the wild waves' perpetual swell,
To depths where monstrous creatures dwell?
  —Yes; for we lay him but to sleep
  Where those blest Feet have calmed the
      deep;
  Little we reck its ebb and flow:
  The Son of Man is Lord also
    Of the ocean.

Leave him with thousand corpses round,
Thus buried in unhallowed ground?
Interred in that same scene of strife,
Where man and steed gasped out their life?
  —Yes; for our King and Captain boasts
  His own elect, His glorious hosts:
  His victors crowned with many a foe.
  The Son of Man is Lord also
    Of the battle.

Why, as across the dewy grass,
Ye, through the evening churchyard pass,
Why welcome in your bells a guest
With chimings, not of woe but rest?
  —Where'er their twilight warblings steal
  We do but ring a Sabbath peal;
  And, till the glorious Sunday glow,
  The Son of Man is Lord also
    Of the Sabbath.

REV. J. M. NEALE, D.D.

'Be of good cheer ; it is I.'—*St. Mark*, vi. 50.

HOLY Scripture saith, 'No chastening for the present seemeth to be joyous, but grievous.' Our afflictions are not blessings *in themselves*. Their mission is like that of the seventy, of whom it is said that Jesus sent them before His face into every city and place '*whither He Himself would come*' (Luke, x. 1). They come to reveal the person of Christ. Before we were afflicted we went astray by looking upon God as an abstract idea or a system of truth; but when sorrow touches us there is a cry within us for the understanding sympathy of a living, loving heart; and this we find in Him who is touched with the feeling of our infirmities, having been in all points tried like as we are.

There is a power for comfort as well as for salvation arising out of the sense of the personality and individuality of Jesus. It is recognised throughout the Gospels and Epistles. Everywhere we find that 'He gives *Himself* to rescue us from ourselves.' St. Peter says, 'Who *Himself* bare our sins;' and the Lord's own words to His affrighted disciples were, 'Why are ye so troubled, and why do thoughts arise in your hearts? Behold, it is *I myself*' (Luke, xxiv. 38).

Let us then look upon our afflictions as the messengers of Jesus, sent before His face to prepare His way. Let us not entertain them with an angry look or frowning brow, but receive them graciously into our habitation, whither we know *He Himself* desires to come, 'who will give us beauty for ashes, the oil of joy for mourning, the garment of praise for the spirit of heaviness.'

IN MEMORIAM.

DEATH's arrows are at random flung,
Or she had never died—so young !
Death cannot choose, or he would spare,
And she had never died—so fair !

Ah ! she was but a twelvemonth's bride,
Not half her love and sweetness tried ;
A mother who had scarcely smiled
Ecstatic welcome to her child.

But yesterday we saw her stand
The centre of a family band ;
Thence called by Love to walk apart,
And fill another's home and heart.

How well she filled that home with gladness,
He knows who mourns its present sadness ;
And how she filled that heart, the token
Is that same heart bereaved and broken.

It seemed as if a rose had died
In all the bloom of summer pride,
And when they whispered 'She is dead !'
I muttered to myself and said,—

'Death's arrows are at random flung :'
But Faith replied, 'The good die young,
Earth's fairest flowers are not too fair
To blossom in celestial air.

The stroke that leaves us desolate
Is not the work of chance or fate ;
'Tis Love that calls its children home,
From wrath and evil days to come.'

GEORGE MORINE.

His will is our peace.
DANTE.

'Forgetting those things which are behind, and reaching forth unto those things which are before.'—*Phil.* iii. 13.

THE precious Word of God has a specific balm for every separate woe. The text before us is meant to meet that special pain we feel in the early hours of bereavement, when we are tempted to linger in thought among 'those things which are behind,' regretting that such and such a course was taken, and wondering why we did not choose a better way, by which the fatal blow might have been averted. There are many folds to our grief, and this is among the most painful. Every heart has known its bitterness; but the manifold grace of God has a special provision for this phase of suffering, in the blessed assurance that our mistakes do not lie outside God's loving purpose for us, but are included in the 'all things' that work together for our good. That chafing regret for the past, which torments us with perplexing thoughts about 'second causes,' is the secret of much of our unrest and misery. It is the 'moth fretting the garment,' the 'garment of praise' which our dear Lord is waiting to give us for the 'spirit of heaviness.' It is confessedly difficult to distinguish between the circumstances which God appoints and those which He *allows*. We cannot charge upon Him those mistakes in our past life which have arisen from the corruption of our nature, yet we may bring them to Him, and believe that His forgiving love is willing to meet and deal with us at the precise point to which those mistakes have brought us. And in all those which have not arisen out of our own fault, there is the unspeakable comfort of knowing that they come to us in the ordering of God's purpose for our eternal gain. When faith is bright we shall perceive that they were only a part of that *garnered* mercy which the Lord has 'laid up for His children,' whereby they might be made partakers of His holiness through that covenant of love which is 'ordered in *all* things and sure,' in and through Jesus Christ our Lord.

IT is Thy hand, my God!
   My sorrow comes from Thee;
I bow beneath Thy chastening rod—
   'Tis love that bruises me.

I would not murmur, Lord;
   Before Thee I am dumb;
Lest I should breathe one murmuring word,
   To Thee for help I come.

My God, Thy name is Love!
   A Father's hand is Thine:
With tearful eyes I look above
   And cry, 'Thy will, not mine.'

I know Thy will is right,
   Though it may seem severe;
Thy path is still unsullied light,
   Though dark it oft appear.

Jesus for me hath died :
   Thy Son Thou didst not spare ;
His piercèd hands, His bleeding side,
   Thy love for me declare.

Here my poor heart can rest ;
   My God, it cleaves to Thee :
Thy will is love ; Thine end is blest ;
   All work for good to me.

From *Hymns selected by* CANON RYLE.

NONE of God's appointments will seem grievous to us if we remember that the *Will of God* never differs from the *Love of God*. If we fear not to rest on the one, we may fearlessly and fully accept the other.

'THINE IS THE POWER!'

THE thought of God's love is, to most of His sorrowing children, the source of their greatest comfort; but there are many who find equal consolation and strength for suffering in the thought of His *Power* as God the Father Almighty, Maker of Heaven and earth. It is a source of comfort given by God Himself in His holy word : ' I, even I, am He that comforteth you : who art thou that thou shouldest be afraid . . . . and forgettest the Lord thy Maker, that hath *stretched forth the heavens and laid the foundations of the earth?*' (Isa. li. 12, 13.)

Even in that deepest sorrow, the sorrow of the forgiven soul for sin, the same reference is made to the glories of creation by the Divine Absolver with a view to encourage our confidence in Him ' He healeth the broken in heart, and bindeth up their wounds : *He telleth the number of the stars, he calleth them all by their names*' (Ps. cxlvii. 4).

It is easy to see how this should be. In the time of our dire distress we are overwhelmed by a sense of our utter helplessness, a feeling which 'the enemy' seeks occasion to deepen into that 'wasting sense of unreality' which may be truly called the orphanage of the soul. Truly, at such times we are come into the 'deep waters,' as the great poet expresses it :—

'In alto mare, senza governo.'*

And as 'deep' only can 'call unto deep,' this anguish is only to be met by a strong faith in a Power infinitely beyond our own : a Power that is not only All-mighty, but All-wise and All-good. We behold the Hand of our Almighty Father conducting all the hidden springs and movements of the universe, and we feel that with the same secret but unerring operation He is directing every event towards the ultimate happiness of His children. Was not this the voice that came to Abraham from out of those star-depths, to whose radiant hosts his attention was directed

* On the high seas, without a rudder.

by God, when drawing forth his faith in the promises of a mighty future for himself and his seed? I think it was. And, blessed be God, there is no speech nor language in the habitable globe where the same voice is not heard. The same stars which spoke to the father of the faithful are over our head now. Let us go forth and stand under those heavens which declare the glory of God, and look upward to that firmament which showeth His handiwork, and let this be our meditation, for such will be acceptable in His sight who is our Strength and our Redeemer.

If the universe has a Father, then *I* have a Father, for whom nothing is too hard, nothing too good, nothing too kind. I will therefore strengthen myself in the Name of my God, and believe that the same Almighty Power that guides the suns in their courses will sustain, guide, and provide for *me*, not only through the brief day of this earthly life, but through the countless ages of eternity.

'MY FATHER!'

ALL things that have been, that are,
   All things that can be dreamed,
All possible creations, made,
   Kept faithful, or redeemed ;

All these may draw upon Thy Power,
   Thy mercy may command ;
But still o'erflows Thy silent sea,
   Immutable and grand.

O weary heart of mine ! shall pain
   Or sorrow make thee moan,
When all this God is all for thee,
   A Father all thine own ?

               FABER.

'THY WILL BE DONE!'

FOUR little words—no more,
   Easy to say ;
But thoughts that went before,
   Can words convey ?

The struggle only known
   To one proud soul,
And Him whose Eye alone
   Has marked the whole,

Before that stubborn will
   At length was broke,
And a low ' Peace I be still,'
   A soft voice spoke.

The pang when that sad heart
   Its dreams resigned,
And strength was found to part
   Those bonds long twined.

To yield that treasure up
  So fondly clasped,
To drain that bitter cup
  So sadly grasped.

And all is calm at last—
  'Thy will be done!'
Enough, the storm has passed,
  The field is won.

Now, for the peaceful breast,
  The quiet sleep;
For soul and spirit rest
  Tranquil and deep.

Rest, whose full bliss and power
  They only know
Who knew the bitter hour
  Of restless woe.

The rebel will subdued,
  The fond heart free;
'Thy will be done'—all good
  That comes from Thee.

All weary thought and care,
  Lord, we resign;
Ours is to do and bear,
  To choose is Thine.

ANON.

FUNERAL HYMN.

HERE, in an inn, a stranger dwelt;
Here, grief and joy by turns he felt:
Poor dwelling, now we close thy door,
    The task is o'er,
The sojourner returns no more!

Now, of a *lasting* home possest,
He goes to seek a deeper rest;
The Lord brought here—He calls away;
    Make no delay,
This home was for a passing day.

SACHSE.

. . ... IN his sufferings the Christian is often tempted to think himself forgotten. But his afflictions are the clearest proofs that he is an object of God's fatherly discipline. Satan would give the man the thing his heart is set on. But God hath better things in reserve for His children, and they must be brought to desire them and seek them. And this will be through the wreck and sacrifice of all that the heart holds dear. The Christian prays for fuller manifestations of Christ's glory and His love to him. But he is often not aware that this is in truth praying to be brought into the furnace, for in the furnace only it is that Christ can walk with His friends, to display, in their preservation and deliverance, His own Almighty power.

CECIL.

ALAS! how sadly do the believer's gloomy spirits under affliction misrepresent before men the love of our gracious Lord! They see, in thousands of smiling faces around them, that health without Jesus can make a man moderately cheerful; and if in us they see that the love of Jesus cannot make a man at least equally cheerful, what inference can they possibly draw but this, that Christ and His love are not nearly so good as the world and bodily health? And is it thus that we expect to persuade the famishing prodigals beside us to leave their swine-husks and to lay hold on our skirts, saying, 'We will go with thee, for we can see that God is with thee?' Let the believing sufferer, then, speak warmly and joyfully of the loving sympathy of Jesus. Let it make his face shine, and his eye sparkle, and his lips drop as the honeycomb. The world counts Jesus an 'austere man,' and formal professors have unworthy thoughts of His harshness, but He looks to us to commend His love. We can do this by lifting our voice in the midst of the furnace, and singing for very gladness of heart, that others, hearing what seems to them a strange song, shall be led to admire the consolation that can so comfort a sufferer; and not to admire it only, but possibly be led to seek it too.

J. D.

IT was not that our love was cold,
That earthly lights were burning dim;
But that the Shepherd from His fold
Had smiled, and drawn them unto Him.

Praise God the Shepherd is so sweet!
Praise God the country is so fair!
We could not hold them from His feet,—
We can but haste to meet them there.

B. M.

IT is a wretched thing to look wearily to Time
alone to blunt our feelings under Nature's ten-
derest grief, and bring a dull forgetfulness of
those whose endeared image should ever dwell
in the brightest chambers of our heart. It is
best—far best, and happiest—to bring the first
full tide of our sorrow to God, and ask Him
to shine upon those waters and change their
nature for us; to lead us along their course to
the clear river of life, at whose Fountain-head
those we love are rejoicing with exceeding joy,
and there to let us in thought dwell continually
with them. Have we not been happy, when in
former times they may have been absent from
us, in thinking of the pleasure they were enjoy-
ing?—pleasure so short-lived, so imperfect!
Can we not be so now, when their happiness is
so great with God, and, like His, eternal? Let
us try to be so; not merely say that it were best,

but really *try* to be so. We can, in a great
measure, if we will; for our moral power is very
great when it rests for its strength on the loving-
kindness, the tender mercies, the faithfulness of
our God.

LADY CATHARINE LONG.

From *Heavenly Thoughts for Morning Hours.*

BODY.

FAREWELL! I goe to sleep; but when
The day-star springs I'll wake again.

SOUL

Goe, sleep in peace, and when thou lyest
Unnumbered in the dust—when all this frame
Is but one dramme, and what thou now descriest
In sev'rall parts shall want a name—
Then may His peace be with thee, and each dust
Writ in His book Who ne'er betrayed man's
      trust.

VAUGHAN.

A VOICE FROM HEAVEN.

I SHINE in the light of God,
His likeness stamps my brow,
Though the shadows of death my feet have trod,
And I reign in glory now.
No breaking heart is here,
No keen and thrilling pain,
No wasted cheek, where the frequent tear
Hath rolled and left its stain.

I have found the joys of Heaven,
I am one of the angel band;
To my head a crown of gold is given,
And a harp is in my hand.
I have learned the song they sing
Whom Jesus hath set free,
And the glorious walls of Heaven ring
With my new-born melody.

No sin, no grief, no pain,—
Safe in my happy home!
My fears all fled, my doubts all slain,

My hour of triumph come !
O friends of mortal years,
The trusted and the true,
Ye are walking still through the valley of tears,
But I wait to welcome you.

Do I forget ?   Oh, no !
For memory's golden chain
Shall bind my heart to the hearts below,
Till they meet and touch again.
Each link is strong and bright,
And love's electric flame
Flows freely down, like a river of light,
To the world from which I came.

Do you mourn when another star
Shines out from the glittering sky ?
Do you weep when the raging voice of war
And the storms of conflict die ?
Then why do your tears run down,
And your hearts be sorely riven,
For another gem in the Saviour's crown,
And another soul in Heaven ?

. . . . LET us sorrow like men, but as *Christian*
men. Let us recollect our many offences against
our heavenly Father—those sins which such a
dispensation may properly bring to our remembrance; and let that silence us, and teach us to
own that it is of the Lord's mercies we are not
consumed, and that we are punished less than
our iniquities deserve. Let those of us who are
under the rod be very solicitous to improve it
aright, that in the end it may indeed be well.
Let us, now God is calling us to mourning and
lamentation, be searching and trying our ways,
that we may turn unto the Lord. Let us review
the conduct of our lives, and the state and
tenor of our affections, that we may observe
what has been deficient and what irregular; let
us pray that through our tears we may read our
duty, and that by the heat of the furnace we
may be so melted that our dross may be purged
away, and the Divine Image instamped on our

souls in brighter and fairer characters. God has made with us an everlasting covenant, and, blessed be His name, we hold not the mercies of that covenant by so precarious a tenure as the life of any creature. It is well ordered in all things, and sure; may it be all our salvation and all our desire; and then it is but a little while and all our complaints shall cease. God will wipe away these tears from our eyes; our peaceful and happy spirits shall ere long meet with those of our children which He hath taken to Himself; our bodies shall sleep, and ere long shall also awake and arise with theirs. Death, that inexorable destroyer, shall be swallowed up in victory, while we and ours surround the throne with everlasting hallelujahs, and own, with another evidence than we can now perceive, with another spirit than we can now express, that all was indeed *well*.

DODDRIDGE.

Oh, the grave! the grave! It buries every error, covers every defect, extinguishes every resentment. There it is that we call up in long review the whole history of virtue and gentleness, and the thousand endearments lavished upon us, almost unheeded in the daily intercourse of intimacy. Ay! go to the grave of buried love, and meditate there. Settle the account with thy conscience for every past benefit unrequited, of that departed being who can never return to be soothed by thy contrition. If thou art a child, and hast ever added a sorrow to the soul or a frown to the brow of an affectionate parent—if thou art a husband, and hast ever caused the fond heart that ventured its whole happiness in thee to doubt for a moment thy kindness or thy truth—if thou art a friend, and hast ever wronged in thought, word, or deed, the heart that confided in thee which now lies cold and still beneath thy feet—then, be sure that every unkind look, every ungraciou word, every ungentle action, will come thronging back upon thy memory and knocking dolefully at thy soul. Then, be sure that thou lie down sorrowing and repentant on the grave, and utter the unavailing sigh and pour the unavailing tear. Then, weave thy chaplet of flowers, and strew the beauties of Nature about the grave. Console thy broken spirit, if thou canst, with these tender yet futile tributes of regret; but take warning by the bitterness of this thy contrite affection over the dead, and henceforth be more faithful and affectionate in the discharge of thy duties to the living.

WASHINGTON IRVING.

ANGUISH is so alien to man's spirit, that perhaps nothing is more difficult to will than contrition. God, therefore, is good enough to afflict us, that our hearts being brought low enough to feed our sorrow, may the more easily sorrow for sin unto repentance.

From *Guesses at Truth.*

BEHOLD, the noonday sun of life
    Doth seek its western bound,
And fast the lengthening shadows cast
    A heavier gloom around;
And all the glow-worm lamps are dead,
    That, kindling round our way,
Gave fickle promises of joy,—
    'Abide with us, we pray!'

Dim eve draws on, and many a friend
    Our early path that blest,
Wrapt in the cerements of the tomb,
    Have laid them down to rest;
But Thou, the everlasting Friend,
    Whose Spirit's glorious ray
Can gild the dreary vale of death,
    'Abide with us, we pray!'

                      ANON.

THE expectation of loving my friends here-after principally kindles my love to them on earth. If I thought I should never know them, and consequently never love them, after this life is ended, I should number them with temporal things and love them as such; but I now converse with Christian friends in a firm persuasion that I shall converse with them for ever. I take comfort in the loss of the dead or absent, believing I shall shortly meet them in Heaven.

BAXTER.

ILL that He blesses is our good,
  And unblest good is ill;
And all is right that seems most wrong
  If it be His sweet will.

FABER.

*　　　*　　　*　　　*

How doth Death speak of our beloved,
　When it has laid them low?
When it hath set its hallowing touch
　On speechless lip and brow?

It clothed their every gift and grace
With radiance from the holiest place,
With light as from an angel's face,
Recalling with resistless force,
And tracing to their hidden source
Deeds scarcely noticed in their course.

This little loving, fond device,
That daily act of sacrifice,
Of which too late we learn the price!
Opening our weeping eyes to trace
Simple, unnoticed kindnesses,
Forgotten notes of tenderness.

Death sweeps their faults with heavy hand,
As sweeps the sea the trampled sand,
Till scarce the faintest print is scanned.

It shows how such a vexing deed
Was but generous Nature's weed
On some choice virtue run to seed.

How that small, fretting fretfulness,
Was but love's over-anxiousness,
Which had not been had love been less.
It takes each failing on our part,
And brands it in upon the heart   .
With caustic power and cruel art.

The small neglect that may have pained
A giant stature will have gained,
When it can never be explained :
It shows our faults like fires at night ;
It sweeps their failings out of sight ;
It clothes their good in heavenly light.

O Christ our Light ! foredate the work of Death,
    And do this now !
Thou Who art Love, thus hallow our beloved—
    Not Death, but Thou !

From *The Changed Cross, and other Religious Poems.*

GOD never shows so much of Himself as in
suffering, and parting with anything for Him,
and denying ourselves of that which we think
stands not with His will. God is no barren
wilderness. One sweet beam of His counte-
nance will requite all this. Wait, then, still
upon God, and He shall shine upon thee.

REV. DR. RICHARD SIBBES.

THE idea of thy life shall sweetly creep
Into my study of imagination,
And every lovely organ of thy life
Shall come apparelled in more precious habit,
More moving, delicate, and full of life,
Into the eye and prospect of my soul,
Than when thou livedst instead.

SHAKESPEARE.

How soothing is the thought that there is no need of constant efforts to urge ourselves to be patient, no need of any strained watchfulness in order to support the character of a virtue which must be constantly acted upon externally. It suffices to be as little children in God's hands, and to surrender ourselves to Him. It is not courage that we need; it is something at once less than courage, and at the same time higher: less in the eyes of even virtuous men, far higher in the eyes of those who judge by pure faith. It is that weakness of self which casts all upon the mighty strength of God. '*When I am weak, then am I strong: I can do all things through Christ who strengtheneth me.*'

From *Christian Counsels.* Selections from Fénélon.

GOD had one Son without sin, but He has no son without sorrow.—AUGUSTINE.

'Thou wilt keep him in perfect peace whose mind is stayed on Thee, because he trusteth in Thee.'—*Isa.* xxvi. 3.

PEACE, perfect peace, in this dark world of sin?
—The blood of Jesus whispers peace within.

Peace, perfect peace, by thronging duties pressed?
—To do the will of Jesus, this is rest.

Peace, perfect peace, with sorrows surging round?
—On Jesu's bosom nought but calm is found.

Peace, perfect peace, with loved ones far away?
—In Jesu's keeping we are safe, and they.

Peace, perfect peace, our future all unknown?
—Jesus we know, and He is on the throne.

Peace, perfect peace, death shadowing us and
    ours ?
—Jesus has vanquished death and all its powers.

It is enough : earth's struggles soon shall cease,
And Jesus call us to heaven's perfect peace.

REV. E. H. BICKERSTETH, M.A.

' Nevertheless, afterward . . . .

Two hands upon the breast, and labour is done;
Two pale feet crossed in rest, the race is won;
Two eyes with coin-weights shut, and all tears
    cease;
Two lips whose grief is mute, anger at peace.
  So pray we oftentimes, mourning our lot;
  God, in His kindness, answereth not.

Two hands to work addressed, aye for His
    praise;
Two feet that never rest walking His ways;
Two eyes that look above, through all their
    tears;
Two lips still breathing love, not wrath nor fears.
  So pray we afterwards, low on our knees,
  Pardon those erring prayers, Father, hear
    these.
                  ANON.

ANCIENT COLLECT.

GRANT us, O Lord, to rejoice in beholding the
bliss of Thy Jerusalem, and to be carried in her
bosom with perpetual gladness; that as she is the
home of the multitude of the saints, we also may
be counted worthy to have our portion within
her; and that Thine only-begotten Son, the
Prince and Saviour of all, may in this world
graciously relieve His afflicted, and hereafter in
His kingdom be the everlasting comfort of His
redeemed. Amen.

WE must all learn to live more in the heavenly
world, with our friends there; and as to the
difficulties of the way, we may lose sight of most
of them by gazing on Him whom all can love,
and trust, and follow.

REV. J. R. BEALEY.

I KNOW not which to choose—whether to live
A little longer here or to depart.
That would be sweet—to be at rest, to toil
No more, no more feel pain; to have no griefs,
No anxious fears, nor for myself nor others—
That would be sweet. And sweeter still to have
No more to sin affection or desire:
But to be near—and feel that nearness— near
Unto my Lord—to have a thrilling sense
Of blessedness, the certainty of joy
At hand yet greater—safe—for ever safe !
A moment since by cruel foes pursued;
Now, nestling 'neath th' everlasting wings,
Conscious and glad of their most tender shade :
So to be resting would be sweet.

And yet,

To live for Christ —to live and do His pleasure,
To fight the fight, clad in His panoply,
Knowing that *He* looks on the while and smiles,
By Love unfathomable ever moved.
To go and tell to others of His grace,

The riches of His wisdom and His truth,
The bliss unutterable of the life
That is in Him : to win them as they lie
Wallowing in sin and dead in trespasses,
To wake and rise and see His glorious sight,
And come to Him and bathe themselves anew
In the all-healing fountain of His blood,
And so be clean and whiter than the snow,
And clothed with Him—the righteousness of
    saints,
Surely a life so spent is blessedness,
And all too little to repay His love—
The love of His most costly sacrifice !
Which shall I choose—living, to live to Christ;
Or dying, die to Him : which shall I choose?
Whichever of the twain shall to Thy glory be,
That Lord, I pray, Thou wilt appoint for me.

REV. H. H. SWINNY.
(*Written a few months before his death.*)

The following beautiful lines from the pen of the late
Dr. Monsell were also written a short time before the
accident which caused his death :—

Wash me, my Saviour! make me pure,
That I Thy presence may endure,
O Thou who from primeval guilt
Didst wash me clean (I know Thou wilt)
To make me for Thy Presence meet,
My head, my heart, my hands, my feet;
From every spot and stain of sin
That lurks without me or within,
Wash in the all-sin-cleansing blood,
Of Thy most pure and precious blood!
Dear body! what more can I do
Than pray this prayer for me and you?
And He will hear it, and will make
Us perfect for His mercy's sake.
You will He render back to dust,
And call me to Himself, I trust,
That we may better serve Him when
Through His dear love we meet again.
And if of death thy happy share
Be resurrection and repair,
Mine—as the sun beyond the star—
Is brighter and is better far!

No knowledge or device thou knowest,
In the still grave to which thou goest.
There thou shalt sleep : the active limb
Shall be relaxed ; the bright eye dim ;
The brain, so quick to understand,
The throbbing heart, the cunning hand,
All must be silent—their work done ;
But I—awake—with Christ shall dwell
In happiness unspeakable !
. . . . Suddenly to ope mine eyes,
And find myself in Paradise !
The gates of death for ever past,
To find myself with Christ at last :
To see that look of welcome given,
Which is the very gate of Heaven :
To feel through all my being move
That holy atmosphere of love :
And, as His hand is on me laid,
Hear these sweet words, ' Be not afraid.'

From *Near Home at Last.*

The writer of the preface to this poem alludes to these
heaven-sent presentiments of approaching death in the
following very beautiful words :—

No doubt there are many examples on record
of the marvellous way in which God, without
disturbing the serenity of the daily life, or bringing a cloud into the sky as visible to others as
the span of a man's hand, does nevertheless
intimate to the soul which He is withdrawing
from the world the near approach of death.
And what a mercy and favour is this to the soul!
What an evidence of the Wisdom which can so
finely adjust a new movement of thought, that it
in no way arrests the order of the previous life,
and yet is making that subtle presentiment so
dominant in the mind that silently, and surely,
and with wonderful rapidity, it is bringing every
activity and faculty of the whole man under its
awful influence! What a niceness of touch,
what tender severity, must belong to the Hand
which can, with the least possible sound, or ex-
citement, or contrast, give such force to the
Invisible as to supersede the Visible, and, without the aid of shadow, bring out the exceeding
brightness of the new heavens and the new earth!

L

NOT sweeping up together,
In whirlwind or in cloud,
In the hush of the summer weather,
Or when storms are thundering loud ;
But, one by one, we go
In the sweetness none may know.

Not passing through the portals
Of the Celestial Town,
An army of fresh Immortals
By the Lord of Battles won,
But, one by one, we come
To the gate of our heavenly home :

That all the Powers of Heaven
May shout aloud for God,
As·each new robe of Life is given,
Bought by the Master's Blood,
And the heavenly raptures dawn
On the Pilgrims, one by one :

That to each the Voice of the Father
  May thrill in welcome sweet,
And round each the angels gather
  With songs on the shining street,
As, one by one, we go
To the glory none may know.

B. M.

DEATH to a good man is but passing, through
a dark entry, out of one little dusky room of his
Father's house into another which is fair and
large, lightsome and glorious, and divinely en-
tertaining. Oh, may the rays and splendours of
my heavenly apartments shoot far downward,
and gild the dark entry with such a cheerful
gleam as to banish every fear when I shall be
called to pass through !

DR. WATTS.

'The Master is come, and calleth for thee.'
St. John, xi. 28.

WE are like to servants
    In their Master's hall,
Busied with our daily work,
    Waiting for His call.

On the roof above us
    Rows of bells are hung ;
One by one they summon each
    With their clamorous tongue.

Then the servant bidden
    Saith, ' That rings for me :'
Leaveth off his present toil,
    Whatever it may be ;

Smootheth his apparel,
  . Looks a farewell round ;
Passeth from his fellows,
    While the bell doth sound ;

Mounteth up the staircase,
    To his Lord doth go.;
Tarrieth in the upper rooms,
    Comes no more below.

Oh, to be up yonder,
Pressing near to God!

Thus we pine and murmur,
Counting service vain;
But the loving Master
Reckons up our pain.

He, the Unforgetting,
Marks our every sigh;
When our hearts are heaviest,
Comfort then is nigh.

When our hope is faintest,
And despair most strong,
And the night-gloom deepens
Round the waiting throng;

Then the welcome summons
Suddenly shall ring,
And our glad steps hasten
To our Lord and King.

ANON.

‘ Pouvez vous mourir tranquille ? ’
PASTEUR T. MONOD.

IF you are Christ's, then Death for you is a
vanquished foe : yea, it does the work of a friend,
introducing you into His presence, where is
fulness of joy. A simple incident shall tell a
world of truth. Not long since an angry bee
flew into a room where a mother was sitting, with
her little child playing by her side. The child
was terrified ; but the bee settled on the mother's
outstretched hand and stung it severely, and left
its sting there, and when the mother showed the
child the sting the little one's heart was at rest :
though the bee was not dead, it was stingless.

REV. E. H. BICKERSTETH.
From *The Shadowed Home.*

FOR so have I known a luxuriant vine swell into irregular twigs and bold excrescences, and spend itself in leaves and little rings, and afford but trifling clusters to the wine-press, and a faint return to his heart which longed to be refreshed with a full vintage ; but when the Lord of the vineyard had caused the dressers to cut the wilder plant and make it bleed, it grew temperate· of its vain expense of useless leaves, and knotted into fair and juicy branches, and made account of that loss of blood by the return of fruit.

JEREMY TAYLOR.

HE wastes nor flower, nor bud, nor leaf,
Nor wind, nor cloud, nor wave ;
And will He waste the hope that Faith
Has planted in the grave ?

HERE on this earth we struggle,
　With toils and cares opprest,
Yet know, through all our journey,
　That ' this is not our rest.'
Our holy Right and Charter
　Is with the saints above,
Our life and conversation
　, Hid with the God of Love.

And though our Lord and Master
　Is gone in Heaven to reign,
We look for His appearing ;
　For He shall come again,
Robed in His sacred glory,
　To bid us dwell with Him
Where all is heavenly sunshine,
　Where light is never dim.

And as His chosen children
　Are called home one by one,
We rest in faith, believing
　That He, the Blessed Son,

With us will one day raise them
  To His eternal throne,
And change our earthly bodies
  All like unto His own.

So, in the faith of Jesus,
  His children dear we laid,
With words of hope and blessing,
  Beneath the church's shade ;
Like forest leaves in autumn
  We fade to things of earth,
But looking for His coming,
  And the new immortal birth.

O glorious consummation !
  O bright unfading morn !
When Christ our Lord shall gather
  His sheaves of full-ripe corn ;
When by His Love and Power
  We near His throne shall stand,
Changed by His mighty working,
  Safe in the Holy Land.

JOHN FABER SCHOLFIELD.

LORD JESUS, from the dimness, the perplexities, the uncertainties of earth, to Thee we turn! While many are speculating and disputing concerning the life to come, questioning of its happiness and of its state, we rest on Thee and Thy sure word of promise. Thou wilt 'receive us to Thyself,' and it will be well; more than this we do not greatly care to know, for we shall be with Thee. We believe, indeed, that the future life will be the perfect flower of which this life is the seed. We know that 'Thou gatherest the wheat into Thy garner,' the corn which we thought was dead: the labours for Thee which seemed to fail—the tender words and cares which we feared were thrown away on earth—the plans for Thy glory which were never realised here—the strivings after a perfect beauty . which should dimly shadow forth Thy divine completeness—the patient searchings for Thy truth in that wondrous book of Nature, as yet but half unsealed to the eye of man—all these things we know Thou art treasuring for us above, until that day when we shall 'rejoice before Thee as with the joy of harvest.'

We know, too, that our dear ones who have slept in Thee are dwelling calm and safe in Thy holy keeping, until the time when God our Father shall bring them back to us with Thee; and we know and are sure that Thou wilt only teach us to love them better in the life to come, because to Thee also they are so dear.

We know that we shall be Thy servants, and serve Thee as we fain would have done on earth; for we shall see Thy face, and Thy Name shall be in our foreheads. But the *manner* of all this we know not, and we would not seek to learn; rather would we have the blessed rest, now, in the thought of Thy coming, as day by day draws nearer the hour of Thine approach—rather the glad surprise at the end, when we shall reach the mansions of our Father's House, and Thou shalt be glorified in us and we in Thee, and God shall be all and in all.

M. E. TOWNSEND.

From *Voices of Comfort.*

'DE PROFUNDIS.'

THE face which, duly as the sun,
Rose up for me, with life begun,
To mark all bright hours of the day
With hourly love, is dimmed away—
And yet my days go on, go on.

The heart which, like a staff, was one
For mine to lean and rest upon,
The strongest on the longest day
With steadfast love, is caught away—
And yet my days go on, go on.

Breath freezes on my lips to moan,
As one alone—not once alone !
I sit and knock at Nature's door,
Heart-bare, heart-hungry, very poor,
Whose desolated days go on.

This Nature, though the snows be down,
Thinks kindly of the bird of June :
The little red hip on the tree
Is ripe for such.   What is for me,
Whose days so winterly go on?

I ask less kindness to be done—
Only to loose these pilgrim shoon
(Too early worn and grimed) with sweet,
Cool, deathly touch to these tired feet,
Till days go out which now go on.

Only to lift the turf unmown
From off the earth where it has grown
Some cubit space, and say, 'Behold !
Creep in, poor heart, beneath that fold,
Forgetting how the days go on.'

A Voice reproves me thereupon,
More sweet than Nature's when the drone
Of bees is sweetest, and more deep
Than when the rivers overleap
The shuddering pines, and thunder on.

God's voice—not Nature's!   Night and noon
He sits upon the great white throne,
And listens for the creature's praise.
What babble we of days and days?
The Day-spring He, whose days go on.

He reigns below, He reigns alone,
And having life in love foregone
Beneath the crown of sovereign thorns
He reigns, the jealous God.   Who mourns
Or rules with Him while days go on?

By anguish which made pale the sun,
I hear Him charge His saints, that none
Among His creatures anywhere
Blaspheme against Him with despair,
However darkly days go on.

Take from my head the thorn-wreath brown?
No mortal grief deserves that crown.
O supreme Love! chief Misery!
The sharp regalia are for *Thee*,
Whose days eternally go on!

For us, whatever's undergone
Thou knowest, willest what is done.
Grief may be joy misunderstood;
Only the good discerns the good—
I trust Thee while my days go on.

Whatever's lost, it first was won;
We will not struggle nor impugn :
Perhaps the cup was broken here
That heaven's new wine might show more clear:
I praise Thee while my days go on.

I praise Thee while my days go on;
I love Thee while my days go on;
Through dark and dearth, through fire and frost,
With emptied arms and treasure lost,
I thank Thee while my days go on.

And, having in Thy life-depth thrown
Being and suffering (which are one),
As a child drops its pebble small
Down some deep well, and hears it fall
Smiling—so I.   Thy days go on.

E. B. Browning.

AN EPISTLE OR HOMILY OF
ST. COLUMBANUS. A.D. 608.

WHAT art thou, O human life? The path art
thou, and not the life of mortals, beginning from
sin and leading unto death. For thou shouldest
have been true had not the sin of the first
transgression broken in on thee, and then thou
becamest vain and mortal, for all that travel by
thee thou dost allot to death. The path art
thou to life, and not life itself. But few discern
thee to be a path—thou art so subtle, such a
deceiver, that it is of few to know thee. Thou
art to be passed through, not dwelt in, O human
life! For a road is not to dwell in, but to walk
on, that they who walk therein may dwell in
their own country. Thou art to be journeyed
through anxiously, cautiously, expeditiously, as
all wise men who are wayfarers hasten to their
true country. We do not seek that on our road
which we hope to enjoy in our country. Labour
and fatigue belong to the road; rest and security

are prepared for us at home. We must, therefore, have a care lest we become careless on the
road, and so come not to our true country. For
some have enjoyed their home on the road, and
with a short life have bought eternal death. Let
us turn aside from earthly things that belong
not to us, that we lose not our own eternal pos-
sessions. Let us be found faithful in the things
that are another's, that we may become heirs of
those that are our own through the gift of our
Lord Jesus Christ. Amen.

HEAVY the trial, because your heart had been
set upon this gift—the more that it seemed so
promising ; but when Patience has had her perfect work, and Faith is once more in exercise,
you will think nothing too good for God, and
you will acknowledge that the choicest, the
fairest, the sweetest of flowers, are fitted for the
bosom of God.

M

'MY AIN COUNTREE.'

I'm far frae my hame, and I'm weary often-whiles
For the langed-for hame-bringing and my
      Father's welcome smiles ;
I'll ne'er be fu' content until my een do see
The gowden gates of Heaven, an' my ain countree.

The earth is flecked wi' flowers, mony-tinted,
      fresh, and gay ;
The birdies warble blithely, for my Father made
      them sae ;
But these sights and these sounds will as nae-
      thing be to me
When I hear the angels singing in my ain countree.

I've His guid word of promise that some glad-
      some day the King
To His ain royal palace His banished hame will
      bring ;
Wi' een and wi' hearts running o'er we shall see
' The King in His beauty' in our ain countree.

My sins hae been mony, an' my sorrows hae
      been sair,
But there they'll never vex me, nor be remem-
      bered mair ;
His bluid hath made me white, His hand shall
      dry mine e'e,
When He brings me hame at last to my ain
      countree.

Like a bairn to its mither, a wee birdie to its
      nest,
I wad fain be ganging noo unto my Saviour's
      breast ;
For He gathers in His bosom witless, worthless
      lambs, like me,
An' carries them Himsel' to His ain countree.

He's faithfu' that hath promised, He'll surely
      come again ;
He'll keep His tryst wi' me, at what hour I
      dinna ken,
But He bids me still to watch, an' ready aye to be,
To gang at any moment to my ain countree.

So I'm watching aye, an' singing o' my hame as
     I wait
For the soun'ing of His footfa' this side the
     gowden gate :
God gie His grace to ilk ane wha listens noo to
     me,
That we may gang in gladness to our ain
     countree.

Do you mourn because God has taken away
your joy? Be glad, rather. He has taught you
how to praise Him, now He will teach you how
to trust Him. This empty time may be the
prelude to higher blessing. After *joy* comes
peace in spiritual gifts. He taketh away the
first that He may establish the second.

ANON.

. . . . WHEN Lazarus died, he 'was carried by the angels into Abraham's bosom' So is it still. Angels gather round the dying beds of believers, waiting until the spirit be set free, that they may bear their charge with songs to its Father's house. Which of us has not heard of saints who, in their last moments, had visions of angels, glimpses of bright faces, and caught strains of richest music, just as heaven was opening its doors to let them in? It has seemed as if some messenger had whispered in their ears, 'The Master is come, and calleth for thee,' for their lips have parted to speak the joyful answer, 'Come, Lord Jesus; come quickly.' We too often think of death as a lonely ex't from the world—a sudden breaking up of all family ties, a mysterious passage into an unknown country, where all will be unfamiliar and strange. But, in reality, it is for the heirs of salvation simply a going home, an entrance into the Father's House, a passing into the happy presence of the Elder Brother, a conscious fellowship with the family above.   REV. CANON BELL.

From *Angelic Beings, their Nature and Ministry.*

FAR out of sight, while sorrows still enfold us,
  Lies the fair country where our hearts abide,
And of its bliss is nought more wondrous told us
  Than these few words, ' I shall be satisfied.'

' I shall be satisfied ! '   The spirit's yearning
  For sweet companionship with kindred minds,
The silent love that here meets no returning,
  The inspiration which no language finds.

Shall they be satisfied? The soul's vague longing,
  The aching void which nothing earthly fills ?
Oh ! what desires upon my heart are thronging,
  As I look upward to the heavenly hills !

Thither my weak and weary steps are tending.
  Saviour and Lord ! with Thy frail child abide !
Guide me toward Home, where, all my wan-
      derings ending,
  I shall see Thee, ' and be satisfied ! '

                              REV. CANON BAYNES.
                              From *Lyra Anglicana*.

. . . . OUR calling is not to interpret provi-
dences, but to trust in promises. God has not
explained to us the profundities of His plans,
but He has clearly revealed the *love of His
heart*. Then let us leave Him to carry out His
own purposes : be it enough for us that we can
count upon His unchanging love.

A young father was once roused from the
first sound sleep of healthy weariness to give
some simple medicine to his child. Scarcely
awake, he took the wrong phial, and did not
discover his mistake till he had given his child
a poisonous dose of laudanum. In great alarm
he hurried to the doctor, and was told that he
had killed his child. The doctor, however,
came to see it, and though he said the case was
about hopeless, they used every effort to save
its life. For weary hours that father, helped by
others, tossed and tumbled and beat with their
open palms the drowsy child, for they were
charged to keep it at all costs awake. If it

should fall asleep, it dies! What a night they
spent! But their self-denying violence of love
was rewarded, for the child still lives, a healthy
school-boy. Now, would we not have wronged
that father's heart if we had judged of it by the
seeming cruelty of his hand? Had we witnessed
his conduct without knowing the reason for it,
we would have been likely to misconceive him
altogether, for the apparent barbarity which
could so shamefully misuse a helpless child
would have shocked us. And yet it was all
done, not in cruelty, but in love—self-denying,
sympathising love. Every stroke he gave fell
on his own heart, and nothing but a most
fervent desire to save the life could have carried
him through the anguish of that dreadful night.

And you, my suffering brother, when God's
outward providence may seem to you to express
anything rather than sympathy, you will still
more grievously wrong your Heavenly Father's
love, and rob your own heart of the comfort
that it needs to strengthen you to patience, if
you foolishly begin to draw conclusions from

what you see with your fleshly eyes in the circumstances of your earthly lot, instead of searching, with anointed eyes, the heart of God as opened up to you in His holy Word.

J. D.

From *The Sympathy of Jesus.*

FATHER, the cup that Thou hast given me,
Shall I not drink it ? Coming from Thy hand,
E'en though at times it prove a bitter draught,
What can it be but mercy ? Nor dost Thou,
Content with giving it, leave it to me
To drink alone ; but as a mother does,
Whose child is sad and sick, Thou drawest nigh,
And with a sheltering arm Thou foldest me
Close to Thy bosom, while Thy other hand
Lifts the cup gently to my shrinking lips,
Mid whispered words of comfort and of love.

THÉODORE MONOD.

'HE KNOWS.'

I KNOW not what will befall me:
God spreads a mist over mine eyes;
At every step in my onward path
He maketh new scenes to rise,
And every joy He sends me
Comes with a sudden and strange surprise.

I see not a step before me,
As I tread on another year;
But the past is still in God's keeping,
The future His mercy will clear,
And what looks dark in the distance
May brighten as it draws near.

It may be the bitter future
Is less bitter than I think;
The Lord may sweeten the waters
Before I come to drink—
Or, if Marah must be Marah,
He will stand Himself by the brink.

It may be He is keeping
For the coming of my feet,
Some gift of such rare blessedness,
Some joy so strangely sweet,
That my lips will only tremble
The thanks they cannot speak.

Oh ! blessed, happy ignorance—
'Tis better not to know ;
It keeps me still in the tender arms
That will not let me go :
It hushes my soul to rest
On the bosom that loves me so.

And so I go on, not knowing—
I would not, if I might ;
I'd rather walk in the dark with God
Than go alone in the light :
I'd rather walk with Him by faith
Than go alone by sight.

My heart shrinks back from the trials
The future may disclose,

Yet I never had a sorrow
But what the dear Lord chose.
So I force the coming tears back,
With the whispered word, ' He knows.'

BRAINERD.

It is well to record here, for our comfort and
encouragement in seasons of depression, when
we are overcome by the dread of a possible
future of suffering, the remarkable way in which
the devout trust expressed in the fourth verse
of this beautiful hymn was rewarded.

In a treatise upon the sufferings of Christ by
a leading divine of the Church of Scotland, in
which the writer contrasts those sufferings in
their fullness and perfection with the sufferings
of His martyrs, which were partially neutralised
by the measure of comfort imparted, we find
these words,—' It is sometimes our Father's will,
in seasons of suffering, to reveal to the spirit so
much of His glory in Christ as neutralises the

physical suffering. *Thus David Brainerd, to whom a very unusual measure of physical pain was appointed, had granted to him along with that pain, when it was most acute, a joy in the Holy Ghost which so counterbalanced that pain, that he judged that condition far happier than an ordinary measure of religious joy with ordinary health.*

Let this recorded instance of God's faithfulness encourage us to leave our future in His hands. 'What time we are afraid, we will trust in Him,' fully assured that if we obey the command to live each day *in* the day, we shall realise not only His 'loving-kindness in the morning' of this our earthly life, but His *faithfulness* also in the 'sight' of death (Ps. xcii. 2).

BLESSING, not cursing, rules above.

TRENCH.

'MY GOD! I KNOW THAT I MUST DIE.'

My God! I know that I must die,
　My mortal life is passing hence;
On earth I neither hope nor try
　To find a lasting residence:
Then teach me by Thy heavenly grace,
With joy and peace to end my race.

My God! I know not *when* I die,
　What is the moment or the hour,
How soon the clay may broken lie,
　How quickly pass away the flower:
Then may Thy child preparèd be,
Through time to meet eternity.

My God! I know not *how* I die,
　For death has many ways to come—
In dark mysterious agony,
　Or gently as a sleep to some:
Just as Thou wilt! if but I be
For ever, blessed Lord, with Thee.

My God ! I know not *where* I die,
  Where is my grave, beneath what strand ;
Yet from its gloom I do rely
  To be delivered by Thy hand :
Content, I take what spot is mine,
Since all the earth, my Lord, is Thine.

My gracious God ! when I must die,
  Oh, bear my happy soul above,
With Christ, my Lord, eternally
  To share Thy glory and Thy love !
Then comes it right and well to me,
When, where, and how my death shall be.

B. SCHMOLK.

RESIGNATION.

'Ich hab' in guten Stunden.'

'What? shall we receive good at the hand of God, and shall
we not receive evil?'—*Job*, ii. 10.

I HAVE had my days of blessing,
All the joys of life possessing,
   Unnumbered they appear !
Then, let faith and patience cheer me,
Now that trials gather near me.
   Where is life without a tear?

Yes, O Lord, a sinner looking
O'er the sins Thou art rebuking,
   Must own Thy judgments light.
Surely I, so oft offending,
Must, in humble patience bending,
   Feel Thy chastisements are right.

Let me, o'er transgressions weeping,
Find the grace my soul is seeking;
   Receiving at Thy throne
Strength to meet each tribulation,
Looking for the great salvation,
   Trusting in my Lord alone !

While 'mid earthly tears and sighing,
Still to praise Thee feebly trying,
   Still clinging, Lord, to Thee ;
Quietly on Thy Love relying,
I am Thine ; and living, dying,
   Surely all is well with me !

      Christian Furchtegott Gellert.

THE room was full of angels,
And she wondered we could not see,
That we could not see their shining wings
As they floated noiselessly
Around her bed.

The room was full of music,
Beautiful music—she said;
And she wondered we could not hear
How the holy strains were stealing,
How the happy songs were pealing,
All through the hush and gloom
Of the silent room.

*   *   *   *   *

And just before the dawning,
When the darkness of night was o'er,
And the night of her suffering life
Was ended for evermore,

In the grey of Ascension morn
The angels came again,
And tenderly they bore her,
For whom they had waited long,—
Watched and waited in heaven,
Knowing that even here
She was learning their blessed song.
So in the grey of morning
They bore her soul away,
Beyond the prison bars,
Beyond the fading stars,
To the brightness of the day.

M. E. TOWNSEND.
From *Voices of Comfort.*

OH most blessed Jesus! perfect God and perfect man, who didst take upon Thee our flesh that Thou mightest unite it to Thy Godhead, let this Thy double nature be to us the pledge of a double mercy. As God, do Thou forget our transgressions; as Man, do thou remember our sorrows. As God, do Thou draw us and lift us up more and more unto Thee; as Man, do Thou return to guide us through the rugged paths which Thou Thyself hast trod in the days of Thine earthly exile. Be with us each moment, in our sorrow and in our joy. Oh Jesu, Divine Master, be merciful unto our sins. Oh Jesu, gracious Friend, sympathise with us in our infirmities. For Thine own name's sake. Amen.

Translated from the French by M. E. TOWNSEND.

JESUS, pity me! I suffer;
  Heavy, heavy is my load,
Desolate my soul within me,
  Dark and rough the lonely road.

Weary, weeping, bruisèd, bleeding,
  Shall I say, Remove the cross,
Take away my pain and sorrow?
  Ah! it were a bitter loss!

Needed cross, and well belovèd,
  My one treasure, dearly bought;
Yet beneath its weight thus fainting,
  Can I serve Thee as I ought?

Saviour, merciful and mighty!
  Gracious help to me impart,
Not by lifting off my burden,
  But by bearing up my heart.

                          ANON.

LOOKING TO JESUS.

'O stilles Lamm !'

' He is brought as a lamb to the slaughter.'—*Isa.* liii. 7.

O SILENT Lamb ! for me Thou hast endured,
Jesus, Thou holy, perfect, sinless One !
Thy grief and bitter anguish have secured
My soul's salvation when this race is run.
    Then let me, to Thine image true,
Thus meekly suffer, with the crown in view.

The narrow way that leads us up to heaven,
Must here through strife and tribulation lie ;
Then, on the thorny path may strength be given,
This sinful flesh, O Lord, to crucify.
    Oh, take this feebleness away,
And make me strong to meet each future day !

If thus we journey patiently through sadness,
Each grief will draw us nearer to our Lord;
But if we flee the cross in search of gladness,
We cannot shun His dread, avenging sword.
  O blessed they who hear the call,
Who take the cross, and follow, leaving all!

So help me, Lord, Thy holy will to suffer,
And still a learner at Thy feet to be:
Give faith and patience when the way is rougher,
And at the end a joyful victory.
  Thus grief itself is changed to song,
Ofttimes on earth, but evermore ere long.

KARL HEINRICH VON BOGATZKI.

'THY WILL BE DONE!'

'It is the Lord : let Him do what seemeth Him good.'
1 *Sam.* iii. 18.

My Jesus, as Thou wilt !
Oh, may Thy will be mine !
Into Thy hand of love
I would my all resign.
Through sorrow or through joy
Conduct me as Thine own,
And help me still to say,
My Lord, Thy will be done !

My Jesus, as Thou wilt !
Though seen through many a tear,
Let not my star of hope
Grow dim or disappear.
Since Thou on earth hast wept,
And sorrowed oft alone,
If I must weep with Thee,
My Lord, Thy will be done !

My Jesus, as Thou wilt!
If loved ones must depart,
Suffer not sorrow's flood
To overwhelm my heart :
For they are blest with Thee,
Their race and conflict won ;
Let me but follow them—
My Lord, Thy will be done !

My Jesus, as Thou wilt !
When death itself draws nigh,
To Thy dear wounded side
I would for refuge fly.
Leaning on Thee to go,
Where Thou before hast gone :
The rest as Thou shalt please—
My Lord, Thy will be done !

My Jesus, as Thou wilt !
All shall be well for me,
Each changing future scene
I gladly trust with Thee.
Straight to my home above
I travel calmly on,
And sing, in life or death,
My Lord, Thy will be done !

B. SCHMOLK.

. . . DEATH does not arrest our influence for good or for evil : it but augments and diffuses it. It travels onward, producing impressions upon the living, lasting as time, ineffaceable as eternity. We leave behind us a vital influence, a living power; flowing through countless, endless channels, the church and the world the better or the worse for our having lived and died. Thus the departed speak to us from the invisible world with a truthfulness we cannot gainsay, and with a persuasiveness we wish not to repel. I hear no voice, see no sign, am sensible of no revelations, and yet there is a spell and a power over me which is too mysterious to explain and too fascinating to resist. It is the spell, the power of undying holiness, strengthened by the solemn sanction and thoughts of heaven and eternity !

Sweet spirit ! thou art near ! Thy gentle presence soothes, thy sacred memory hallows, thy present glory allures me : and to follow thee as thou didst thy Lord, and to be with Him as thou art, shall be the guiding-star of my being.

REV. OCTAVIUS WINSLOW, D.D.

THOUGH not yet
The dead sit up and speak,
Answering its call, we gladlier rest
Our darlings on earth's quiet breast,
And our hearts feel they must not break.

Far better they should sleep awhile
Within the church's shade,
Nor wake until new heaven, new earth,
Meet for their new immortal birth,
For their abiding-place be made,

Than wander back to life and lean
On our frail love once more.
'Tis sweet, as year by year we lose
Friends out of sight, in faith to muse
How grows in Paradise our store.

Then pass, ye mourners, cheerly on,
Through prayer unto the tomb;
Still as ye watch life's falling leaf,
Gathering from every loss and grief,
Hope of new spring and endless home.

From *The Christian Year*.

. . . . LET all those who suffer endeavour to shake off *self*—to throw aside a selfish sorrow, without faith, without love, and consequently without consolation, and to enter fully into the love of Christ, that their sorrow also may be like a cross planted in the earth, under the shadow of which all those that surround them may take shelter, not to receive eternal life, but to learn the way that leads to it, to the glory of God. To Him be glory for ever and ever! Let us rejoice in Him, and be well assured that by the power of faith and love there is no sorrow that ought not to be peacefully and joyfully supported, and made to subserve to the glory of God, to the good of mankind, and to our own eternal consolation.

From *Adolphe Monod's 'Farewell.'*

'The former things have passed away.'—*Rev.* xxi. 4.

THUS we see that earth's tears are the prelude
to heaven's joy. John the Baptist was in the
desert till the day of his showing unto Israel,
and our blessed Lord passed forty days in the
wilderness before His ministry began. And it
is always so. The reaper's gladness must be
prefaced by the sower's tears—the rainbow's
colours must be wrought in the weeping cloud.
Every feast has its vigil of fasting and solitude.
The Song of Songs is ushered in by the lament
of Ecclesiastes. This is the law of life. Yea,
life itself is one long vigil to that high festival
of the regeneration of all things, when the
'former things' of waiting, watching, praying,
and weeping, shall have passed away, and all
things have become new.

AFTER DEATH.

Oh, where exists the spirit world,
　　Which we must some day surely see?
Oh, where abides the Paradise
　　In which no death can be?

That mystic, solemn, sacred world,
　　Where every eye is free from tears,
And every hand is true and good,
　　No fallings, and no fears?

The world where we may hold for aye
　　Treasures far dearer than we lost;
Live on in blithe eternal peace,
　　Be no more tempest tossed?

Will there be tranquil meadow trees,
　　Broad-bowering in their leafy calm?
And gentle winds that sleep through noon,
　　And wake for evening psalm?

Will there be sunshine on vast hills,
   And rivers in the spreading vales,
And wealth of flowers, and dewy lanes,
    Where flute the nightingales?

Will there be gardens whose sweet fruits
   Ripen and redden all the day?
And homes where clustering roses cling,
    And do not fade away?

We know not; but the weary fight
   Is over where that world shall be,
And changed the aching of the soul
    To calm felicity.

O Lord of Life, our hands are full
   Of Thy sweet gifts; we judge Thy love,
To those who love Thee, will be shown
    In fairer forms above.

But what the sounds that we may hear,
   Or what the sights that there may be,
Thou knowest, O Sovereign of the skies,
    And we can wait to see.

SORROW leaves sacred responsibilities. When
God takes away our dear ones He does not
intend that we should merely weep and suffer
loss, trusting to time for healing—shall we say,
forgetfulness?—and living lives unaltered by the
tears we shed! The heaven into which our
beloved ones have entered comes very near to
us in our great sorrow. We hear its songs, and
see its white-robed company. Earthly things
take a second place in our hearts, and things
spiritual are seen to be eternal realities. We
rouse ourselves to inquire what revelation has
to tell us concerning that unknown shore, and
concerning those heart-yearnings for reunion.
Shall we suffer feelings like these to pass away,
leaving no impress upon our lives? We do so,
alas! too often, and thereby we lose those great
chances for good which God gives us through
the ministry of sorrow. The fault lies chiefly in
our imperfect apprehension of spiritual truths,

which is the result of a feeble grasp of God's
word. That word reveals to us the state and
condition of the blessed dead, under every
possible analogy of earthly joy and of human
thought and feeling. But, through indolence
and earthly-mindedness, we see it not. Friend
after friend departs, and we discern not their
blessedness, and remain uncomforted and unblest ourselves. Who has not felt his miserable
unreality on this subject? It is indeed as
common as it is sad to hear Christians confess
under bereavement that they do not believe in
the recognition of saints. Some go so far as to
say it were wrong to do so. Their beloved is
gone, and gone for ever ; they have a vague and
confused notion that he is safe with God, but on
a shore so remote, and among an assembly so
vast, that it were vain to hope for recognition and
reunion. Do not such Christians weep, indeed,
' as do others who have no hope ?' Meanwhile
their own lives are unreal and without aim ; for
where is the energy for duty, for self-discipline,
and for suffering, where the sanction for human

O

love and joy, if death is not only to interrupt
but to put an end to it all?   Let such mourners
lay aside their prejudices and take the comfort
that God sends them in His holy word.   Let
them not merely read, but *study* that word ;
comparing all those passages which refer to the
condition of the dead in Christ.   Let them
mark the description given of the heavenly
Jerusalem in Heb. xii., and ponder those wondrous visions of St. John which reveal to us
bright glimpses of the heavenly Temple with its
worshippers.   They will then see that the present
state of God's blessed saints is not one of sleep,
but of holy, active joy, of loving service, of rest,
and of grateful adoration in the presence of
Jesus; that their sins are washed away in the
atoning Blood of the Lamb, and that, released
from all guilt, and freed from every stain, they
are 'without fault before the throne of God;'
that they are not *isolated* in the midst of that
vast multitude which no man can number, but
are associated as brethren with the 'general
assembly and church of the first-born ;' that their

spirits are made perfect in the full development
of every faculty and power which had its progress
in this life ; and further, that these faculties and
powers are now under heavenly training for
future service and future glory in the regenerated
earth (Rev. v. 10). To this add another feature
of their heavenly condition, most comforting to
their bereaved friends on earth, that they *are
not unmindful of their former life.* The 'kindred'
and 'tongue' and 'people' and 'nation' are
remembered in the song of those worshippers
who ascribe praise to the Lamb slain. And it
is not too much to infer also from other passages
that they are interested in all that concerns our
spiritual welfare, and (most comforting assurance!)
that they love us still.* Who shall rob us of
truths so cheering and heart-consoling, so long
as they are sanctioned by God's word, which is
infallible truth ? Who shall say that they have
not the highest practical tendency, that we may
not in them find the strongest motives to a life

* On this subject see *The Intermediate State of the
blessed Dead,* by the Rev. Dr. Baylee.

of faith in the Son of God, and of greater diligence to make our 'calling and election sure?' They would supply us with new motives, new energies, for the race that is set before us. This earthly life of ours would become more and more real, in proportion as we see it is one with the heavenly and spiritual world—one in its training and discipline—one in its human affec- tions and the ties which bind heart to heart.

God give us grace to discern His glorious purposes towards the Church of His redeemed— to ponder them—to pray over them, until our lives catch something of that glory which shines out to us like stars through the darkness of this mortal life !

'O Almighty God, who hast knit together Thine elect in one communion and fellowship, in the mystical body of Thy Son Christ our Lord; Grant us grace so to follow Thy blessed saints in all virtuous and godly living, that we may come to those unspeakable joys, which Thou hast prepared for them that unfeignedly love Thee : through Jesus Christ our Lord. Amen.'

'They sing as it were a new song before the throne.'
Rev. xiv. 3.

THE lonely watch of life is o'er,
And yonder, hand in hand,
The 'bright-faced kindred' stand,
All griefs forgot, on Canaan's shore.
Redeemed from sin and shame,
Bearing the Father's name,
The Lamb they follow evermore.

They sing aloud before the throne ;
That song, for ever new,
To them so sweet, so true,
Can no man learn but they alone.
How should the song of joy,
Of Love without alloy,
By sinful heart on earth be known ?

All things are new in that blest clime,
The sweet and pleasant air
Grows never chill—for there

No cloud o'ershadows morning prime ;
   Upon the summer sky
   No deepening shade may lie,
No darkness follow evening chime.

The song is new ; for earthly things
   Have passed away—the pain,
   The grief of human stain.
And now, beside the living springs,
   They joy and know no fear,
   They love and shed no tear,
They soar and know no weary wing.

Be patient, then, though joys be few,
   Sad heart ! a little while.
   Canst thou not wait His smile ?
Canst thou not trust His promise true—
   Who share My cup of pain
   With Me shall drink again,
When Heaven's wine is made anew ?

For the Sick and Sorrowful.

A Book of Sympathy and Comfort for Bereaved Parents.

1. Our Lambs in the Fold Above.
Selections by LADY DUNBAR. With Photo Frontispiece.
24mo. cloth, 2s. 6d. ; leather bindings, 3s. 6d. to 10s.

'It has been an ingenious thought which has induced Lady
Dunbar to gather many voices of comfort for bereaved parents into
one short manual. The choice has been discriminating, and will
commend itself to sorrowing hearts.'—*Christian Observer.*

2. Songs in the Night.
Or, HYMNS OF HOPE AND TRUST FOR WEARY WATCHERS.
Selected and Arranged by ANNA CLOWES.
Extra crown 8vo. very large type, limp cloth, 2s. ; paper cover, 1s. 6d.

'Will no doubt prove a welcome companion to many of those who
are afflicted or distressed.'—*Record.*

3. The Sheltering Vine.
Selections by the late COUNTESS OF NORTHESK.
Introduction by the Most Rev. R. C. TRENCH, D.D.
Archbishop of Dublin. Ninth Thous. Two Volumes, 10s. 6d.
Volume I. 6s. ; Volume II. (on Loss of Friends), 4s. 6d.

4. The Name of Jesus, and other Poems.
By C. M. NOEL. 14th Thous. Sq. fcap. 8vo. cloth, 2s. 6d.

5. Words of Peace; or, The Blessings of Sickness.
By BISHOP OXENDEN. 61st Thou. Fcp. 8vo. *large type,* 1s. 6d.

6. The Home Beyond ; or, A Happy Old Age.
By BISHOP OXENDEN. 138th Thous. Fcp. 8vo. *large type,* 1s. 6d.
This Volume bound with 'Words of Peace,' roan, 5s. ; mor. 7s. 6d.

7. Words of Consolation, Pardon, & Hope.
By Author of ' Words of Mercy and Peace,' &c.
14th Thous. Fcp. 8vo. very large type, limp, 1s. ; in packet, 6d.

'Very suitable for the poor and sick. Thoroughly evangelical,
earnest, and faithful.'—*Sword and Trowel.*

HATCHARDS, PUBLISHERS, PICCADILLY, LONDON.

YEAR-BOOKS OF TEXTS.

The Soul's Inquiries Answered
in the Words of Scripture.
By G. WASHINGTON MOON, F.R.S.L.

NEW DRAWING-ROOM EDITION. Small crown 8vo.
On special Writing-paper, with 13 Copyright Photographs.
Cloth extra, 10s. 6d.; roan, 13s. 6d.; mor. 17s. 6d.; extra, 21s. to 42s.

'A very beautiful birthday-book. . . . Each month is prefaced by
an exquisite illustration of some incident in the life of Christ, from
well-known paintings by modern artists. Few handsomer gifts of
the kind could be given or received.'—*Standard.*

NEW POCKET EDITION. With Diary. 23rd Thousand.
32mo. cloth, 2s., 2s. 6d.; roan, 3s., 4s.; morocco, &c. 6s. to 42s.

CHEAP EDITION. Square 24mo. Without Diary.
Limp cloth, 1s. 6d ; roan, 2s. 6d.; morocco, &c. 7s. 6d. to 10s.

COMMON EDITION FOR DISTRIBUTION.
Without Diary. Square 24mo. limp, 8d.

Sacred Trichords;
Or, Corresponding Texts from the Old and New Testaments,
with a Verse of Sacred Poetry between, in harmony,
for every Day in the Year. 32mo. cloth, 2s. 6d.; circuit, 3s.

'Carefully and well selected. . . . . Each saint's day and holy
day has been specially considered in the selection of verses.'
Church Bells.

A New Daily Text and Hymn-book for Children.
Words of Love for the Little Ones.
Selections by L. A. MORRIS. With Photo Frontispiece.
24mo. cloth, 2s. 6d.; gilt edges, 3s.; leather, 3s. 6d. to 10s.

'Heartily do we commend this little volume to the attention of
mothers.'—*Mothers' Treasury.*

HATCHARDS, PUBLISHERS, PICCADILLY, LONDON.

www.ingramcontent.com/pod-product-compliance
Lightning Source LLC
Chambersburg PA
CBHW030826020726
47499CB00006B/2086